ADV.... ....,eD:

"Georgia scribe Benji Carr isn't just breaking down barriers with his bullet train of a novel, *Impacted*, he's kicking them in with steel-toed boots. Carr takes the modern thriller to a higher level that challenges the reader to step out of their comfort zone and grab the tail end of a goddamn lightning bolt. Novels like *Impacted* are not written to be fodder for pop culture, then put back on the shelf. They are written to blow open the status quo, like a chunk of literary C4, and force the reader to think — while their heart pounds harder and faster with every turn of the page. If a new and fiercely original voice in fiction is something that interests you, try on some Benji Carr. *Impacted* knocked my dick in the dirt. And I'm sure this is just the beginning."
— Brian Panowich, award-winning author of *Hard Cash Valley*, *Like Lions*, and *Bull Mountain*

"Like a shot of novocaine, Benji Carr injects his novel with enough pitch-black comedy to take all my pain away. *Impacted* had my jaw on the floor, either from laughter or sheer gob-smacking shock. Pray that you remember to grab your own mandible back up once you've finished reading this hilarious debut novel."
— Clay McLeod Chapman, author of *Whisper Down The Lane* and *The Remaking*

"You could read Benji Carr's edge-of-your-seat novel as a thriller, with all the twists and gut-punches you crave. You could read it as a kind of *Rashomon* deep dive into the lives and moral choices of a cast of characters who might seem like you and me…but, trust me, who aren't. But the surest way to appreciate what Carr manages in this riveting debut is to see in *Impacted* a coming-of-age story unlike any you have read before. You might not quite believe what young Wade Harrell lives through in just twenty-four hours but, once you finish the book, you're not likely ever to forget him."
— Jonathan Rabb, author of *Among The Living* and *The Berlin Trilogy*

"A darkly comic novel by a wildly talented new voice. For better or for worse—I'll never go to the dentist again without thinking about this book."
— Colleen Oakley, *USA Today* bestselling author of *You Were There Too* and *The Invisible Husband Of Frick Island*

"*Impacted* is a wise, wicked noir that will set your teeth on edge. Benji Carr has some seriously dark and funny chops."
— Andy Davidson, author of *The Boatman's Daughter*

"Benji Carr's mesmerizing debut novel, *Impacted*, a thriller wrapped up in a coming of age, is a heartfelt cautionary tale about secrets and lies, the ties that bind and those we get bound up in. You will root for the sensitive, befuddled protagonist Wade, who is having a rough time juggling the responsibilities of new fatherhood, mourn-

ing his own father, and being thrust into exploring his sexuality. In swift punchy prose, Carr has written an unputdownable novel about exploitation and how easily a life can derail and the ways in which second chances become possible, or not."
— Soniah Kamal, award-winning author of *Unmarriageable*

"Wade Harrell is the kind of protagonist you want to slap some sense into before giving him a hug and some words of wisdom, except none of us, hopefully, has ever faced the hilarious and outrageous problems that author Benji Carr keeps throwing at Wade. So the best advice for Wade might be 'Good luck, and don't do anything stupid!' Of course, Wade won't listen. Carr's darkly comic yet heartfelt storytelling allows us to laugh at Wade while also empathizing with him, and the perspectives of other characters help us better understand Wade and remind us that, while everyone struggles one way or another, it's better to struggle together than on our own."
— Christopher Swann, author of *Never Turn Back*

"A consistently surprising, twist-filled, emotionally resonant treat! I never knew a trip to the dentist could be so insanely entertaining!"
— Jeff Strand, author of *Pressure*

"The characters are outrageous, intense, and totally believable, and the story keeps you riveted till the end. It was a pure delight to read."
— Jessica Nettles, author of *Children Of Menlo Park*

IMPACTED

IMPACTED

BENJI CARR

The Story Plant
Studio Digital CT, LLC
P.O. Box 4331
Stamford, CT 06907

Story Plant paperback ISBN-13: 978-1-61188-305-3
Fiction Studio Books E-book ISBN: 978-1-945839-52-8

Visit our website at www.TheStoryPlant.com

First Story Plant Printing: July 2021

Printed in the United States of America
0 9 8 7 6 5 4 3 2 1

Wade turned off the ignition on the off chance that it somehow saved him gas, though he had no idea how the inner mechanics of a Prius worked. Wade didn't have his dad's know-how. Wade knew nothing. So much nothing. What happens when a smart kid learns nothing useful? He ends up waiting to speak to better men who know how to do things, waiting for them to notice him. The hanger-on. The shadow. The pest.

Why was he even there? What did he really want to do with this man? Was it another rendezvous or a reckoning?

"You think too much," the doctor had told him, right before their first lunch break. It started during Wade's lunch breaks from work, this "friendship."

Maybe he should just go inside the office. He could charge his phone, at least, while he was waiting. It wouldn't be the first time. Wade should just walk in. Nobody in there would care, after all. Most people in that whole damn complex beat it at 4:45 p.m. His assistant Celeste even left early from the office on Wednesdays to get her son. He would just look like another patient, the last patient of the day. No one would care—except Dr. Emmett. Dr. Emmett might rage. And shout. And push Wade against a wall. And leave bite marks. That would be worth it.

The jackass was keeping him waiting. Wade opened the car door, then removed the key when his Prius noticed some unfinished business and started dinging at him.

All Wade could think about was Dr. Emmett, who rattled around his head every day having imaginary conversations with him. Sometimes his version of Dr. Emmett whispered something to him, sometimes the version shouted. The best thoughts of Dr. Emmett were memories: that day they went to the lake, the time he only wore his lab coat, how he always had lollipops in his pocket. Sometimes, in Wade's head, Dr. Emmett was just mad or annoyed or puzzled. Wade couldn't tell how Dr. Emmett actually felt.

When Wade reached the office, it wasn't locked, but there was no one manning the front desk. He took a breath and entered. Dr. Emmett's waiting room had those cream-colored sofas that had phone chargers embedded into their armrests, the ones that were USB-ready. Dr. Emmett bragged on his furniture, saying those seats had been a real hit with the customers. Sometimes they didn't even mind the wait. Time on your phone is time in your head. Time in your head passes at a different speed than real life. Wade plugged in the phone and its cord, then laid it face down on the chair. He didn't sit. He stood at the center of the waiting room, taking in the view.

Dr. Emmett's office wallpaper was a full New York skyline. Standing at the center of the lobby was supposed to make you feel on top of the world. Dr. Emmett told him they could go anywhere if things were different. Wade wanted to believe him.

But we exist in suburbs, Dr. Emmett. We could walk to a Kroger from here. Escape is momentary, even from the lies we tell ourselves. A dentist's office is intended for pain. We can numb ourselves to it, cover it in a shiny veneer, but all the pretending is a lie. Happiness isn't possible here. We just fuck around with each other and fuck each other up.

The speakers blared some soft rock or something. The clock on the wall read 5:37 p.m.

Wade's eyes narrowed, alongside his patience. His mind raced. What exactly was forbidden about being in Dr. Emmett's office? His back teeth were floating, as well. So he opened the door out of the waiting area and made his way to the unisex bathroom down the darkened hallway with Chicago along its walls, feeling his way along the counters. Wade helped himself to a mint. His fingertips grazed the braces on a ceramic mouth model. Then, he heard a mutter come from an exam room on the left, then some giggling. Light, airy giggling, as though Dr. Emmett didn't have anyone waiting on him.

The exam room door was open only a smidge, but the bathroom was right next door. So, Wade entered the bathroom, pulled the knob before shutting it so that there was no click, no sign that he was anywhere he shouldn't be.

Wade listened at the wall, feeling terribly old-fashioned, before biology reminded him of his actual reason for being in the bathroom. He unzipped his fly, then took aim against the side of the bowl, praying that one drop would not betray him. He wanted to eavesdrop, not dribble. He listened to see what was occupying Dr. Emmett's time, which was supposed to be their time together. Perhaps a patient needed an emergency crown. Maybe the laughing gas was leaking, and everyone was in danger, and Wade could save them. Maybe it's good that he was there, sneaking around his lover's office.

It was his duty to listen. His bladder empty, Wade stayed put, sitting on the commode, ear to the wall again. Who gives a damn if it's old-fashioned? Wade listened closely for the reason he'd been ignored.

On the other side of the wall, Wade's answer came.

Dr. Emmett's voice sounded annoyed, desperate. He was pleading with someone.

"... No, I need you to listen to me for once, damn it. I'm tired of going over this," Dr. Emmett said. "Are you gonna... Hello... Hello??"

Wade heard Dr. Emmett slam his fist down on his desk.

"Oh, for fuck's sake," the dentist shouted. "Fucking hold again... You suck, Daphne!"

The dentist hit a key on his phone, then slammed down the receiver. A light, cheery symphony filled the air.

Taking quick advantage of the moment, Wade stood from the toilet, exited the bathroom for the Chicago-lined hallway and then said, in as innocent a tone as he could adopt, "Hello...??? Hello???!!!"

He meandered slowly down the hallway, as though it was the first time he'd been here.

"Wade? ... Wade, what are you—" Dr. Emmett called.

A moment passed. A button clicked. The symphony died. A brief rustling came from the exam room, then Dr. Emmett poked his head into the hallway.

"Wade, it's so good to see you," Dr. Emmett said without smiling, but he didn't move from the doorway. "But I thought you were going to wait in your car. I should only be a few minutes."

Wade glared at the older man, noting the wrinkles in his brow. Dr. Emmett could be worried. Dr. Emmett could be angry. Real Dr. Emmett was such a mystery, unlike the Dr. Emmett who wandered across Wade's mind every day. That one nibbled at him, taunted him, kissed him. Wade had no idea how to read this real Dr. Emmett.

Wade approached the dentist inch by inch, walking past John Hancock toward the Sears Tower as though he were covering the actual blocks.

"Dr. Emmett, it's been an hour I've been outside," Wade said calmly. "I saw your last patient leave already. Some lady and her son, right?"

Dr. Emmett nodded but came no closer.

"An hour, sir," Wade repeated. Wade dropped his head in disappointment, he didn't blink. "You summoned me here, and you kept me waiting an hour."

"I'm sorry, Wade."

"Why?" Wade blurted.

"I'm sorry I kept you waiting, Wade," Dr. Emmett muttered. "I guess that was rude."

"You guess?"

Dr. Emmett rolled his eyes and changed his approach. His demeanor shifted toward menace, and he finally stepped out of the doorway, toward the counter.

"Whatever. You're here now. In my fucking workplace."

Wade bristled.

"I had to use the bathroom, sir."

Dr. Emmett stepped closer to Wade, then past Wade. Then he opened the damn door back into the lobby for

Wade, waving for him to follow. Like it was nothing. Like they didn't have plans. Like he was just dismissed. Like it was so easy. Like Wade was disposable. Wade, dumbstruck, just stood there. And eventually Dr. Emmett had a tone.

"Well, Wade, now that you're finished, could you leave my office before someone sees you?"

Wade's eyes widened.

"Who the hell would even see me? You're here alone."

"We have cameras. We have security guards. And, more important than all of that, I have boundaries that I already told you, Wade."

"We met here, Dr. Emmett," Wade asserted. "You're my damn dentist. Why the fuck couldn't I just need an emergency crown or something? It's conceivable that I'd be here."

Dr. Emmett's veins bulged in his forehead.

"Listen to me, Wade," he said. "If you don't leave here right now, you're going to need a goddamn emergency crown."

Wade was stung, but he didn't back down.

"I thought you liked my mouth this way," Wade said.

Dr. Emmett smirked, not about to be outsmarted, "You can tell people that just as easily as I can, Wade—which is why I know you won't."

"I could cause a lot of trouble for you, Doctor."

"You can't threaten me, Wade," Dr. Emmett said. "You have too much to lose. Just go."

"Why'd you keep me waiting if you just want me to go?"

Dr. Emmett paused. "It's not like there's anywhere you have to be, Wade. Your whole life is spent just filling time."

"What?" Wade said, approaching the counter, trying to steady his sudden nerves.

"Go home, Wade. I'm not in the mood for you right now."

Dr. Emmett hit the light switch outside his office, illuminating the hallway where they stood. Wade's eyes squinted, the blue of them sparkling in the track lighting.

"There," Dr. Emmett scoffed. "Now you can see your way out."

Wade recoiled, turned toward the lobby, then couldn't motivate himself to just walk away from the good dentist.

"Doc, will I hear from you tonight?" Wade wondered. "I mean, if you're more in the mood to talk later."

"I don't think so, Wade," Dr. Emmett said. "You crossed a line."

Wade was unsure exactly how he had crossed one. He'd dated people before. He'd gone to see them at work. It hadn't been a big deal. It certainly wasn't a make-it-or-break-it situation. Granted, Dr. Emmett wasn't like anyone Wade had ever been with in many ways. The fact that he found him attractive at all had been surprising. Dr. Emmett had been so persuasive in the beginning, when Wade was so confused.

Once again, Wade was confused, and Dr. Emmett was so certain.

"Look, I don't get this," Wade confessed, still afraid to look at the dentist. To look at him, it might be over. *Over* over. "I never know where I stand with you."

"You don't stand anywhere with me, Wade."

The office phone rang.

"I really have to get that," the dentist said. "You interrupted me before."

Dr. Emmett walked behind the reception desk and picked up the line. He eyed Wade's back, and Wade started to go away.

"Yes, Daphne, hello," Dr. Emmett muttered into the phone, his tone more chipper and professional. He turned away from Wade and leaned against the counter. "Did you and the good folks ever track down where my damn sofa is? Or do I have to wait another full day for delivery?"

Wade froze.

"Daphne, I don't want to hear any excuses," Dr. Emmett said. "My time is valuable, and I can't just be waiting around for you like a putz."

Enraged, Wade turned, huffed and grabbed the ceramic mouth model up off the counter. The jawbone connected to the back of Dr. Emmett's skull before he got out another word. Wade felt the crack more than heard it. The dentist slumped to the ground behind the desk.

Wade looked down upon his lover. With the mandible firmly in his grasp and with Daphne saying "Hello... hello...," he walked through the lobby and out the door. Wade reached the Prius, opened the door, tossed the teeth into the passenger seat. Then, he took another swig of the tea, which was cold now. And Wade drove away, the engine barely even purring as the car exited the parking lot.

CHAPTER TWO

THE RIDE HOME WAS TEN QUICK MINUTES. Wade spent the first of them dazed, unsure of what to think of what had just happened. Denial was numbing. He couldn't look in the passenger seat at the mouth, afraid of the smile it might return to him if he looked. The thing hadn't felt really heavy in his hand, unless Wade didn't know his own strength. Maybe it was made of plastic. Maybe Dr. Emmett was just fine, actually. Wade was tempted to look at the gums, the bicuspids, the molars, the wisdom teeth. Perhaps there was blood staining the teeth now. Maybe his weapon had gingivitis. His fears wouldn't recede. Perhaps Wade should just distract himself.

The only CD in the car was full of lullabies for the baby, which usually he avoided listening to unless Lydie was in the car with him. He glanced in the rearview at her car seat, out of habit. It had been a hard habit to learn, yet now he couldn't help but do it. Thinking of Lydie or about Lydie led him to check the rearview. Of course, the car seat was empty when he looked. Lydie was at home, probably with her mom or even with his mom. Maybe Lydie was holding the bottle with her hands. His Lydie was such a cute little girl. And she was getting so big. Two months already? Things go so fast.

Why hadn't he been thinking of Lydie when he clobbered Dr. Emmett? What had he done?

How much more could he screw up his goddamn life?

Good God, I have a kid, Wade reminded himself. Then, he grabbed the burned CD from the console, desperate for a distraction. "Songs for My Grandbaby" was sprawled across it in red Sharpie, written in his mother's handwriting.

"Lullaby and good-night, go to sleep now, my baby...," some syrupy sweet chirpy singer crooned softly within moments. "All is love, yes, all is love..."

Wade winced. Where had his mom gotten this shit? Usually, the woman had better taste than this. Was she trying to give Lydie terrible taste? This was the sort of music used in hostage negotiation. Was this some sort of passive-aggressive way of punishing him for all the times he'd misbehaved? Is Kidz Bop just some kind of grandparent voodoo magic?

It droned on, though it did not lull him or distract him, for Wade's mind was always wont to wander. His thoughts meandered from the baby to the song to how tired he felt all the time to love to sex to, *damn it, are the brakes squeaking?* to *could I fall asleep right now? What the hell is happening?* The music was not helping.

He hit the stereo screen, putting the CD to a stop. Maybe he could listen to his audiobook or a playlist or something. Wade couldn't think about the baby now. The young man couldn't think of how violent he had been or where that violence had come from and that no one would understand. Two minutes 'til home, maybe he'd be able to finish another chapter of that

Norman Vincent Peale thing he'd been slowly working through.

Wait.

Wade took his right hand off the steering wheel. He checked his pocket. No. Other pocket. No.

He looked at the passenger seat. That fucking grin, it gleamed white. No blood that Wade could see. No cavities. Shiny and ceramic, the mouth mocked him. It hinged open like one of those wind-up novelties. The mouth laughed at him.

The mouth was the only thing in the passenger seat. Wade could see no cell phone, no charger cord.

Panicked, Wade pulled to the side of the road abruptly. Indeed, the brakes did have a squeak.

But he had no phone. And his memory of where it was played out before he could stop it. The New York skyline. The couch with the built-in charging stations. The furniture that Dr. Emmett was so in love with. Furniture that he cared about more than Wade, furniture that he doted on and waited for. Furniture that was expensive and valuable, things that meant something to the good dentist. Wade was cheap to Dr. Emmett. Wade was worthless. Dr. Emmett would yell at Daphne, but then he just turned away from Wade. Dr. Emmett couldn't even muster enough anger to scream at him. Dr. Emmett just turned away, like Wade was nothing.

Wade's cell phone was on the couch in Dr. Emmett's office. He had to turn the car around. There was no other option. He looked out the window, checked his rear-view. There was no Lydie in her car seat. There was no oncoming traffic. He eased the blue Prius into a U-turn and drove the eight minutes back to the place he'd rather never see or think about again.

Δ

Once that familiar parking lot came into view, Wade slowed the car to a crawl. Though he'd been there less than 20 minutes before, even though he'd been there loitering several nights a week for two months, it felt like a different place, no longer safe or comfortable. He crept toward it, easing into the left turn. Because of his trepidation, cars passed him on the right. Wade kept expecting one of them to be a cop car. That'd just be his luck.

Someone honked at him. It broke him out of the stupor, and he pulled into the parking lot.

Wade realized, as he made his way toward his usual spot between the dentist's office and the frame store, that the building wasn't the trouble. He was the trouble. He'd been careless. He'd been dangerous. Now, he needed to be more careful. And far more dangerous. Wade needed to be a man now—the way men were in old movies and cop shows. He needed to be that way—a man and a dad—for Lydie. Not being that way only leads to secrets. And secrets only lead to trouble.

He parked and stared at the building again. There were no other cars there, except for Dr. Emmett's. He wasn't just waiting. He wasn't just scared. Wade needed a plan. Not having a plan makes everything go to shit, so he needed to come up with a plan, just in case. Wade also needed to psych himself up before he returned to the scene of his crime.

"You have to get that phone, Wade," he muttered to himself, thinking like a good coach and then behaving like one in a locker room at halftime by raising the volume on his command. "YOU HAVE TO GET THAT PHONE, WADE! GET HYPE, WADE! GET THAT FUCKING PHONE!!"

He paused, looked in the rearview at himself, and then admitted, "Oh my God, I'm nuts." Wade didn't feel like a killer. Wade felt like a kid.

He had to go into that office and grab his damn phone. His life would be over if anyone found it. There was too much stuff on it, too many secrets. Texts and photos between him and Dr. Emmett. Wade had sent Dr. Emmett all sorts of photos, at the man's request.

Suddenly, he remembered that phones worked both ways, and his plan became more complicated. Could he get both phones?

In truth, Wade never wanted to look at the good dentist ever again. But he also wanted to see his daughter grow up, not just during monthly visitation to the penitentiary. Maybe he could get both phones.

Wade realized he'd been there three whole minutes before he urged himself out of the seat. He still couldn't look in the passenger seat and face the teeth.

He opened the driver's side door and swung his legs out quickly. The Prius dinged at him, reminding him to turn off the headlights he'd forgotten about. As he pulled himself out of the car, he turned the knob 'til the sidewalk in front of him was only illuminated by the dusk. He looked at his watch. It was 6:30 p.m. Someone had probably been texting him by then.

Δ

Wade opened the door to the waiting room, looked again at the New York City skyline along its walls. Two quick steps inside, and he had his phone and charger cord in his hand. He yanked the cord out of that fucking electric couch, taking his anger out on the dentist's damn furniture.

Four missed calls. Ten texts. All from home.

Wade was torn over whether to try and get Dr. Emmett's cell phone. He tried to think over his mom's favorite crime dramas, whether the phone records could be retrieved even if he destroyed the dentist's cell. His mind wandered from "SVU" to "CSI" to "NCIS: LA" before it landed on, of all people, Edward Snowden. Then he thought of Trump and Russia. Damn it, Wade realized, modern technology fucking sucks. It's useless to try and hide anything, unless you're the President of the United States and can just break whatever law you damn want and step on anyone who gets in your way.

It would do no good to destroy Dr. Emmett's phone. The cops would have the information anyway. Wade was screwed. The government already had his dick on file in some NSA warehouse. Best to just get away from this place before he left more evidence. His fingerprints were all over this place. Had he touched Dr. Emmett's body this visit? He hadn't.

And then another memory hit him. It overwhelmed him. Wade hadn't flushed the toilet.

He couldn't just stand here, even though part of him just wanted to freeze. Wade bolted very quickly from the New York lobby to the Chicago hallway, not bothering to look behind the nurses' workstation where Dr. Emmett lay. Wade didn't need to see that again.

Just pretend this isn't happening. Just flush the toilet. Just go.

Wade went in the bathroom, flushed the commode and bolted back past the Chicago skyline as quick as he could go. He glanced over toward Dr. Emmett for a moment, daring himself to see what he'd done, but all he could glance were the man's loafers before, with a deep breath, Wade was once again safely in the New York lobby.

He walked to the front door, started to push it open and realized, in horror, that someone else was pulling it open from the other side. Suddenly, Wade stood eye to eye with another guy, who looked just as confused to see him in the office.

CHAPTER THREE

"HEY, SORRY TO KEEP Y'ALL WAITING," THE GUY SAID TO WADE, CON-TINUING TO PULL AT THE DOOR. "Are we still good to go?"

Wade kept his hand on the door, but this man's fore-arms bulged, making himself more room, until Wade gave up the resistance. The guy smiled when he realized Wade was no longer blocking his entry. He looked Wade up and down.

"Thanks, kid," the delivery man said.

Wade scanned the guy, trying to get his bearings. The man was, luckily, a quick study.

There was a clipboard in his other hand. He wore a blue jumpsuit with a delivery logo on it. The man's name was sewn on to the chest.

TREVOR. Dark hair. Green eyes. Olive skin. Firm build. Maybe 19 or 20. He smelled of Old Spice. Wade was standing too close to him.

"Anyway, like I said to dispatch, we were having real difficulty finding this place," Trevor said. "Must've passed by it like four times. The sign out front is too damn small, if you ask me, and it just says DENTIST. No-body's name or anything. I thought it would be in an of-fice complex, not a strip mall."

Wade wasn't in the right mindset for this. Trevor's eyes sparkled. A bit of chest hair peeked out from the top of his uniform. Trevor just kept talking. Wade felt cold sweat on his forehead. There is a body in the next room, Wade thought to himself. There is a body in the next room, and you have to get the hell out of here.

"So, do you know where he wants it? It should fit through this door." Bingo.

"Oh," Wade said. "You're here with the sofa he was talking about." Trevor nodded.

"Daphne, the lady at dispatch, told me that he was still waiting here for it," Trevor said. "But there's a problem."

"A problem?" Wade asked, wondering if he should just run. But Trevor was bigger than him.

"Yeah," Trevor said, taking in the New York skyline. "Nice wallpaper. So, like, is Dr. Emmett here? Daphne said he was real particular."

"He's gone," Wade said. His pulse quickened at the words.

"Oh," Trevor said. "Man. What gives?"

"The office closed."

"But Daphne said he was waiting on us," Trevor said. "Look, can I just bring the couch in? You can sign for it, and, that way, we don't have to come back here."

Wade froze.

"I really don't know where he would want it," Wade said.

"So, are you like his son or something? If you're 18, I think you can sign for delivery."

"I just turned 17, actually," Wade admitted. He had just turned 17.

Trevor regarded the young man a moment.

"You look older," the delivery man said to the dangerous, panicked teenage father who, just then, did feel so much older. "You look my age. When was your birthday?"

"Last week."

"Happy birthday, Aquarius," the delivery guy said, then he winked.

Wade shivered. There was a moment. And then Wade imagined how much of Dr. Emmett's blood was on the floor of reception.

Trevor switched tone, eased himself into the room. The door shut behind him.

"Look, I doubt this is going to actually matter, but could you sign for this sofa?" he asked. "I'm already here."

"I really don't think I—"

Trevor glared at him, wanting to get this done with minimal difficulty. "But, if you're his son, I think I can still have you sign for the delivery."

Trevor lifted the clipboard. Wade put his phone in his breast pocket.

"It isn't a big deal," he urged it forward.

A pen dangled from a chain off the clipboard. Wade grabbed it and scribbled Wade and an E Something Something on to the receipt, maintaining the ruse.

"So, it's Wade?" Trevor asked. Then Trevor wrote a date and time next to the signature. Wade watched him do it. Then, Wade looked over his shoulder to the hallway door.

"I really have to go. Is that cool?" Wade asked.

Trevor scoffed at this, then raised an eyebrow.

"No, I actually have to deliver the sofa now."

"Can't you guys just bring it in?" Wade asked.

"That's what I'm saying, there's a problem," Trevor complained. "My other guy is back at Burger King. He wanted me to find the place while he grabbed food for both of us."

"Well, that was stupid," Wade said. "Dr. Emmett was already waiting."

"Your dad, right?"

"Right. My dad was already waiting."

"But he left?" Trevor asked.

They were both trapped in an Abbott & Costello routine, and Wade hated himself every minute that passed. Life was never not complicated, never not going to be complicated, never going to be any fun, never going to be free. It was stupid. He was stupid. All of this was stupid.

Wade's voice went sharp and insistent.

"Yes, damn it, he is gone. I told you he was gone already, and he's gone. House call." Trevor opened the door and began to step outside.

"Well, not to make you saltier, but then you're going to have to help me carry this thing, kid," the delivery man said.

Wade followed Trevor's lead out the door. Wade wanted God to strike him dead right there, just unleash lightning from the sky. It might be the only way to escape this. Wade didn't even have time to think.

Wade's phone vibrated against his chest. He was expected home by now. But Trevor didn't need to see anything but the lobby of the office. He didn't need to see

Dr. Emmett on the ground. Trevor didn't need to call the cops. Trevor didn't even have to know he'd walked into the middle of anything at all. Trevor opened the hatch of the delivery truck, lowered the ramp, then climbed inside the trailer by putting his feet on the bumper instead. His suit tightened around his muscles as he moved. Wade looked over Trevor, in spite of himself.

Damn it, Wade thought, I get turned on as often as a light switch. I've got a fucking body in the office and a kid at home, and I'm ogling a delivery guy who could be moments away from destroying my entire life.

Trevor walked around the bright sofa, wrapped in plastic, and faced him. He dropped the clipboard in the trailer and kept his eyes on Wade.

"Can you get yourself up here, or do you need a hand, Wade?"

As usual, when faced with someone more assertive, Wade did as he was told. Everyone in his life was more assertive than Wade Harrell. He approached the back of the truck, and Trevor offered an arm to steady him and lift him up.

"Nah, man," Wade said, but Trevor grabbed a hold of him anyway. Wade was swept up into the trailer in a controlled, graceful manner.

Wade blushed, which made Trevor blush.

"I just—Sorry, I just—I just move a lot of furniture," Trevor stammered. "It's just easier for me to grab hold of somebody."

Wade thought about the last time he blushed at a man. And he thought of that man's body on the floor in the office. And he moved away from Trevor toward the end of the sofa.

"Let's just get this over with." Wade grabbed the end of the sofa and lifted from his knees, the way his dad once taught him. His actual dad, not Dr. Emmett.

Trevor's smile dropped. He became matter of fact, echoing Wade's tone. He grabbed the other end of the sofa and walked toward the ramp.

"It's better if I go backward," Trevor said. "I do this a lot. I'm used to it. My name's Trevor, by the way."

"Yeah," Wade said, "I can read." He nodded toward the shirt. Trevor's forehead wrinkled as he wondered where he went wrong. Even dumbstruck, Trevor was handsome. Wade had no time for it.

The sofa was cream-colored, short. It didn't have the charger stations within it, so Dr. Emmett probably meant for it to go somewhere other than the lobby. But Wade didn't think Dr. Emmett would care at all where it ended up now. This sofa cost him his life, in a way. All Dr. Emmett had to do was just not keep Wade waiting, but this sofa was so damn important. So now it was going in the wrong place to spite the dentist, who'd been picky with his furniture yet careless with the people in his life. For other, more obvious reasons, this sofa was only going to the lobby. The delivery guy was never leaving Wade's sight.

The sofa was easily carried down the ramp, down the sidewalk, to the doorway.

Trevor gently placed his end of the sofa down to open the door and tried to make more small talk.

"Is that your Prius?"

"Sure."

"It looks new. Was it a birthday gift from your parents?"

"Nah," Wade scoffed. "They can't afford something new. I got it last year before Lyd—" Wade cut himself off.

"I mean, I just keep up with it, wax and stuff," he said. "It's not new. I work at the grocery store."

"Your dad can't afford a Prius?" Trevor asked, incredulous. "I guess dentists don't make what I figured."

Damn it all, Wade thought.

Δ

Soon, the sofa, Trevor and Wade were inside Dr. Emmett's waiting area. The sofa was planted awkwardly in a corner. And Trevor just waited for Wade to say something. And waited.

"What?" Wade asked him. "You're looking at me funny. Is there something on my face or something?"

Trevor moved toward one of the couches, as though he were about to sit down. Wade moved toward the door and opened it for the guy. Trevor didn't budge.

"Don't you have to go get your buddy from the Burger King, Trevor?" Wade asked him impatiently.

"I honestly have no idea," Trevor said. "My phone's dead. I was gonna ask you if I could charge it here."

He pointed to the same charger station where Wade had left his phone.

"You can use my phone to call him if you want," Wade said anxiously. "But we gotta go."

From the reception desk, a folder of papers fell to the ground, startling them both. Wade turned from the New York room to the Chicago one, waiting for another noise.

"I thought you said your dad was gone," Trevor said.

"He is," Wade said.

"Well then, what was that?"

"What was what?"

"Something fell back there," Trevor said.

Wade's life was over. Trevor would call the police on him. He'd never see Lydie again. His parents would hate him. His church would disown him. His whole family would have to move out of town to escape the scandal.

"Probably just papers," Wade said. "The receptionist is really disorganized."

Wade forced a smile. He kept walking out the door. Trevor, hesitating a moment, followed him.

"Do you have keys?" Trevor asked once they were outside, the sky now dark.

"My dad said he's coming back here, actually," Wade said. "He can shut down everything, set the alarm, see the receptionist's mess for himself. I have somewhere to be."

Wade grabbed his own keys and hit the unlock button on the Toyota fob. He rushed to the car.

"Wait a damn second, Wade," Trevor barked as Wade opened the car door.

Wade froze again. Trevor walked slowly toward him, a look of alarm on his face.

"You're forgetting something important," Trevor said expectantly.

"Huh?"

The car door standing open between them, Trevor reached over to Wade, his hand extended. Wade didn't know what was coming, something tender or terrifying.

And Trevor's fingers touched Wade's shirt, reached into his breast pocket and grabbed Wade's phone. Wade sighed in relief.

Trevor took the phone, turned away and typed a quick text.

Turning back, he announced, "—and send."

Then he handed Wade back the phone. Wade glanced down at the phone screen. The text to 678-555-5519 said "OMW."

As Wade looked up, Trevor was already walking away.

The delivery guy climbed into his truck, and Wade followed suit into the Prius. He made sure that Trevor was gone, in the direction of the Burger King, before Wade headed home himself, eager to finally get the hell away from Dr. Emmett's office. It was past 7 p.m.

All the way home, he listened to Norman Vincent Peale's guidance and prayed for his soul's forgiveness.

CHAPTER FOUR

WADE KILLED THE HEADLIGHTS BEFORE PULLING INTO THE DRIVEWAY AT HIS HOUSE, HOPING TO DELAY ANYONE FROM NOTICING HIS ARRIVAL BEFORE HE HAD A CHANCE TO COLLECT HIMSELF. It was 7:45 p.m. All he wanted to do was go to sleep. But he knew that wouldn't be happening. His phone had been blowing up the entire drive home, which led him to keep putting on the brakes. The Prius took the last available slot on the concrete. Everyone was there. There would be no peace.

Still, the young man took a breath, stepped out of the vehicle without regard for the mouth in the passenger seat, and went through his usual arrival routine.

The house on Sycamore was a split-level blue one with white shutters. His parents bought it about 12 years ago, getting it during a foreclosure auction. He'd had the same bedroom from the age of five until he brought his own child home last year. Then, his mom had the basement finished and moved him down there. That way, he and his girlfriend Jessa could take care of Lydie on their own. And, as a side benefit that she never expressly mentioned out loud to him, his own mom wouldn't have to look at him as often. As he passed by the front of the house, though, she made an exception and pulled back the curtains. He glanced up at her. The look expressed her usual disappointment. Wade turned away from it, feeling dread.

He used to be able to come to his mom with any problem. They'd been especially tight since his dad died. But that hadn't been the case since Jessa got pregnant. Wade had to be more selective, though their relationship seemed normal, even playful. He couldn't tell his mother that most days he felt like dying, that he was trapped by circumstances that never entirely felt caused by his own choices. He couldn't tell her anything troubling ever again. He'd lost that right. He couldn't tell her anything about Dr. Emmett before, and he sure as hell wasn't mentioning a damn thing about it now to anyone.

From the driveway, he walked around the front of the house toward the fence gate. He opened it, then walked along the stepping stones toward his own "front door," leading into the basement. It wasn't locked.

He turned the knob, pushed it slowly open and was immediately hit with a delightful sight. Jessa was dancing with their daughter in her arms to some girl power-ish pop song on the radio.

Seeing him, her green eyes widened, and she smiled. But there was concern in her tone. "We've been worried sick," Jessa said, indicating the baby in her arms. "The heck have you been?"

"Practice," Wade said.

"Which one?"

Just like everything else in his life, Wade couldn't keep his lies straight.

Jessa wore a smirk, some faded blue jeans, and a T-shirt with a small floral pattern. It was sweet, a little country. With her strawberry blonde hair in a ponytail and a face decorated with freckles and sun, she looked very much like the girl he had passed notes with when he was 10. It was no mistake that she looked like Sissy Spacek in old movies. Jessa aspired to it. Jessa was a huge fan of old movies, and she loved Sissy Spacek movies where she was sweet and innocent one minute, murderous and cunning the next. Jessa always aspired to toughness. She wanted to be a badass, and, over the course of the past year, she had managed it.

When her preacher dad found out she was pregnant, Jessa told Wade that she needed a place to stay. She didn't ask Wade if he wanted the baby, thinking of that as something he should've considered before they had any sort of sex at all. Before Lydie showed up, he resented it. He resented that life had to change so dramatically and so quickly. Wade wished he could only consider sex in terms of punishment, for it was far more grief than it was worth.

He and Jessa weren't even dating when it happened. They were just, like, friends. They'd known each other for a long time but weren't really close. Then, once, while he was having the worst day, she started talking to him at church about fried chicken. They sat next to each other in French class one semester and played Tic-Tac-Toe whenever the teacher went to smoke. As soon as Madame Lively headed for the door, Wade would turn toward Jessa's notebooks and cross four lines in the corner of one of her pages. She'd roll her eyes at him. He knew she hated a ruined blank page. But she'd still put down an X every time. And they'd talk about movies. Or about their dads. Or about Wade's bullies. Or just random gossip about which cheerleaders had drug problems.

But all the mistakes brought him Lydie. And nobody who knew her was angry about Lydie, not even his mother.

Jessa used to say that, if her parents would only just let their guard down and see their granddaughter, they'd feel blessed to love her. But Rev. Lancaster wouldn't budge. Since he kicked Jessa out of the house, he wouldn't even take her phone calls.

She would tell Wade that her dad cared more about his congregation and the gossip of little old ladies than he did about family. This surprised her. She always viewed her dad as this tower of strength, but towers fall.

Strong men fail. Weak boys fail. Jessa deserved better. Wade knew that.

Wade's girls were so pretty, the family so beautiful. Wade was overwhelmed. He didn't know what the hell he was doing tonight. Or with his cock. Or in his whole damn life. Wade started shaking, the tears hitting him with a shock. Jessa saw it, and he quickly tried to regain control of the feelings. There was no way to tell her anything. His life was much too fragile. He had to keep lying.

Jessa eyed him suspiciously.

"You OK? You seem a million miles away," she asked.

"I'm sorry, I just—," Wade said. "I was getting food after practice, and my phone died. I had to wait to charge it."

Already, Jessa was on to the next thought.

"Can you take her?" Jessa asked, handing over Lydie. "My arms are tired. She's getting so big."

Not waiting to be handed, Lydie lunged with a smile toward her daddy. Wade caught her, thinking the girl fearless. He envied that boldness. Wade didn't feel bold, not even when he clobbered a dentist over the head. In that moment, he was angry and desperate.

Wade looked to his girlfriend, held his daughter and tried to maintain his composure.

"Mom didn't give you any grief, did she?" he asked.

"Only a little," Jessa said. "You should've been here to grab Lydie sooner, like we talked about."

"I know," Wade grumbled.

Jessa's pretty green eyes narrowed. Her tone of voice grew firm.

"No, I'm afraid that's not good enough. I need you to more than 'know.' I need you to 'do,' Wade. Your mom needs it too. Lydie needs it."

Wade glared at her, and her shine started to fade. No one was constant.

"And don't whine," Jessa said. "I don't, so you can't."

Well, I don't know about that, thought Wade. Jessa wasn't perfect. She was guided by whims, most of which she picked up from off TV, and it had actually led them to their situation. But Betty probably said something to Jughead about "not whining" on tonight's episode of "Riverdale" or whatever. So now he was getting lectured.

Jessa was like that, existing on a steady diet of teen drama and vampire romance. She suggested their casual hookup after spending a week binge-watching "The Vampire Diaries." Her favorite characters were Klaus and Caroline.

"Everyone thinks we're already doing it," Jessa had told him that Friday night last March, whispering to him while he tried to watch some Billy Wilder movie she'd picked from his dad's collection. "Don't you kind of want to get virginity out of the way?"

"What?" he asked her. She'd come over to watch some old DVD every Friday for about a month. Wade would make microwave popcorn. They'd done two Hitchcock and a Robert Wise, and that night Jessa picked a murder mystery.

"People think we're dating," Jessa told him, causing him to glance away from Marlene Dietrich, whom Wade had never seen before.

"Who?" he snickered.

"People at school."

"That's weird," he said. "I hear different gossip."

Jessa didn't let him finish the movie that night. Wade still didn't know whodunit, besides them.

The baby fidgeted. Jessa excused herself to go do some homework, so Wade sat with the baby on their hand-me-down couch and flipped through the channels. His stomach growled.

He moved toward the kitchenette, putting Lydie on the floor at his feet. He searched the one cabinet.

"Hey Jessa? Do we have any chips or anything?"

"No," she called from their bedroom. "I thought you ate already."

Wade's stomach remained empty, though his mind began to fill with worry. He needed to be better at covering his tracks. Though he'd never killed anyone before, he'd certainly seen enough episodes of "Murder, She Wrote" on the Hallmark Channel with his mom growing up. A plan would help.

Δ

At 9:47 p.m., according to their little white microwave, Wade headed up the basement stairs to try and raid his mother's pantry. Lydie slept in her crib while Jessa typed some essay in their room, and he knew he'd have to embark on the guilt trip his mom had planned for him eventually. Might as well get it over with and get some Pringles or something, Wade reasoned.

The steps squeaked as he approached the basement door, and he knew his mother would be on him within minutes. He went to the pantry, sifted past some Lorna Doones toward the good Girl Scout stuff. He grabbed a box of Cheerios, as well, because he knew otherwise that she would ask if the cookies were all he was going to eat.

When he stepped out of the pantry, Mary was already surveying the choices in his arms.

"You're gonna gain weight," she said. "You shouldn't be eating this late. It just stays on your stomach all night, and you never burn it off."

"I could stand to gain some weight, don't you think?"

"You could stand to gain some damn muscle, not a gut," she said. "Just trust me on this."

"I know, I know," the son said to the mother. "You're a professional."

"Wade, I'm an LPN! You make it sound like I work for Weight Watchers." His eyes widened over the shock of the idea.

"God forbid," he said, opening the Thin Mints box and grabbing a whole sleeve. Then, he opened the sleeve, knowing he was antagonizing her while refusing to say anything. He slowly unpeeled the plastic, knowing the noise of it was just making his mom anxious. Within moments, she scoffed and headed to the fridge. Mary grabbed the milk.

"You cannot eat those cookies without milk, Wade!" she announced. "I raised you better than that."

She poured him a full Solo cup, better for dipping, and passed it to him. "So, what's been going on with you?"

Wade faltered and lied, "Just school, you know."

"I don't, actually," Mary said. "That's why I asked. We don't talk as much as we used to."

"It's nothing, really," Wade said. "Just trying to juggle all the stuff."

Mary glared at her son, assuring he could feel the judgment. She let the silence hang in the air.

"Go on," he said. "I know I screwed up tonight. You can just tell me."

"I'm not supposed to be the one picking Lydie up from daycare, Wader," she said, making the reprimand sound almost cute. "I have too much to do at the hospital. When my shift ends at 6, I just want to go home."

"I know, Mom."

"Knowing doesn't seem to make you actually do the right things, Wade," Mary said. "Instead of knowing something, do me a favor. Damn do something."

"I lost track of time after school," Wade said.

"Doing what?" she asked him.

Wade had no answer.

"Where were you, Wade? Hanging out with those kids at the store again?"

"I work there, Mom."

"Yes," she said. "And you shouldn't be loitering outside of the grocery store, waiting to talk to bagboys or whatever, on a day when you're not supposed to be there. It's unprofessional. It's irresponsible. And you have a daughter you're supposed to be grabbing from daycare."

"Mom..."

"Today was your day, Wade," she said. "Today was YOUR day together."

"I know."

"I'm going to need you to step up. I feel like I've done a lot for you and Jessa and Lydie. You have your own space. You both were able to stay in school. You didn't need to worry about daycare."

"I know, Mom."

"I don't think I ask for much," Mary said, returning the milk to the refrigerator.

"Of course, you don't think that," Wade muttered.

Mary glared at her son.

"You forget yourself," she said. Then she sighed and walked away from him. "I need sleep. So, do you."

And Wade tried to remember all the things he'd forgotten or lost today: his phone, his patience, his senses, his temper. His mind wandered to the false teeth in the front seat of his car. He considered going to get them, but his mom would notice his exit, maybe even follow him out the door to see if he was leaving again.

Unsure of the right course of action, Wade, perplexed, did nothing about the teeth. He crammed the cookie tube back into the box, returned it to the pantry, and went back downstairs to his bed.

When he entered his bedroom, Jessa was already under the covers. She eyed him expectantly, as though she were Veronica ready to pounce Archie Andrews.

He shook his head and said, "No, I'm spent." He asked her to turn off the lamp. Then Wade tried his damnedest to actually sleep.

CHAPTER FIVE

THE RACING, PARANOID THOUGHTS KEPT WADE FROM SLEEPING SOUND- LY THROUGHOUT THE NIGHT. He kept waking up, gasping, over- come by the scope of the mess he'd created. The gasping would startle the baby for a moment, so he had to keep still so that Lydie and Jessa wouldn't be bothered. It was still a weird sensation for him to have to share a room with anyone. He wished he could undo all of it, grateful as he was for Lydie. He wished she'd come along when he was ready, when he was out of school. But there was no way to erase what had happened.

When sleep would fail him, Wade would try to plan how to get away with murder. But he wasn't good at that. He could find trouble. He couldn't solve it, like an adult would. He wasn't an adult. In his imagination when he was awake and in dreams when he wasn't, visions of Dr. Emmett kept taunting him.

"You stupid fucking baby, thinking you can kill me," he imagined the dentist whispering in his ear, lying in the bed next to him instead of Jessa. "You're trash. You're nothing. You will suffer the rest of your life for this."

Wade had to whisper to himself that it wasn't real, that there was a way through this. It's what Norman Vin- cent Peale told him every day in that audiobook. He shut his eyes, trying to sleep again.

Wade thought about how things started with Dr. Emmett two months before, how his choices led him to this nightmare. And then he considered further to the first time he met Dr. Emmett. In a way, his mom introduced them. He was the closest dentist she had for in-network insurance coverage.

Δ

A week before Christmas, just after Lydie was born, Wade started getting these headaches, and they wouldn't go away. His mom joked that it was just being a new parent and that the headaches never completely leave you, even after your kids start having kids of their own. But Wade swore that wasn't it.

"This isn't stress," he complained to Jessa while they were wrapping presents that night. "This aches. It pulses, and it aches. I can't believe my mom thinks this is all some damn joke."

Mary was a nurse, after all. Wade couldn't understand why she wouldn't suggest anything more than an Advil and an ice pack. His mom seemed to alternate between fierce protection and severe anger over all the problems that her son brought to her doorstep, and he couldn't predict which ones would set her off.

"I just don't get it," he muttered.

But Jessa wasn't listening to him. She kept staring at the Advent calendar that she bought, muttering vague agreements to him like "Uh huh..." when he reached a stopping place in his rant.

Wade glared at her and then tested her.

"Maybe Santa Claus will get me what I want for Christmas," he said to her.

"Uh huh," she replied.

"Someone who actually gives a damn about me," he spat.

At that, Jessa turned and said, "Maybe he'll do the same for me."

"Goddamn it," he shouted. "What the fuck is even your problem right now?"

Jessa shook. Her eyes took on a spirit Wade had never seen.

"You wouldn't understand."

"I hate when you do that," Wade said. "I asked you to explain something that's clearly bothering you, and then you just clam up. What the hell?"

"You are my problem right now," Jessa shouted. "You. You. You."

"What did I do?"

"You got me pregnant, jackass," she growled. "You ruined my whole damn life. And you don't even care."

"I wasn't the one who wanted to have her," Wade replied. He immediately regretted it. "I wasn't even the one who wanted to do it. That was all you."

Jessa scoffed.

"It was all you," he repeated.

She took a breath and then continued in a calmer tone.

"I have never missed a Christmas concert in my life," she confessed. "The whole church comes together, every

49

choir of every age group, and I have never, ever missed it. Usually I even get to sing a solo."

"Was it tonight?" Wade asked.

She threw a roll of wrapping paper at him.

"Yes, you damn idiot," Jessa shouted. "It was tonight. And my parents didn't even call me. They haven't even seen our baby. They said the congregation wouldn't even welcome me in the doors if I ever showed up again."

Wade gritted his teeth, angry for her and angry at himself. And that's when the pain truly started, as though someone was stabbing him in the mouth. He buckled over, screaming. His mouth filled with blood.

Δ

The next morning, Wade drove himself to the emergency appointment alone, one hand on the steering wheel, the other holding an ice pack to his jaw. Though he had not slept, the pain kept his eyes open while the Prius made its way down the road. No one was willing to drive him or stay with him. After putting him in his upstairs bedroom for the night and raiding the first aid kit for all its gauze, Mary made the call to get the appointment scheduled, but she had to work at the hospital the next morning. In an act of sheer bitchiness, Jessa, still mad as hell over church, over the baby, and over every damn thing, told Mary that she would drive him, but changed her mind as soon as Mary was out the door. So, Wade drove himself to Dr. Emmett's office, wincing all the while. He made his way into the empty waiting area and approached the front desk window, tears in his eyes and an ice pack in his hand.

"Can you help me?" he asked weakly, tears welling in his eyes. "I'm Wade Harrell, and I have—"

As he spoke, he struck a nerve. Wade couldn't help it. He moaned.

Celeste, her braids tight and long, her skin dark, had her eyes down in a folder. As she looked up at him, her expression went immediately from kindness to terror.

"Baby, you're in pain," she said. "Come back here immediately. That ice pack ain't going to help at all."

She rushed to the door, shouting for Dr. Emmett to come out with the Novocain already because some poor boy was white as a ghost. Wade wandered from the New York waiting room to the Chicago hallway.

And so, Dr. Emmett rushed into the scene, needle in hand. The dentist was primed for emergency, and Wade sat on the couch and opened his mouth for salvation. Soon, his mouth was numb, and his eyes clouded over. In that moment, Dr. Emmett seemed like the most beautiful man he'd ever seen.

"It's OK, Wade," Dr. Emmett said. "I'll take care of you."

And he entwined his arm with the boy's, guiding him into the exam room. Celeste was at Wade's other side, helping them along.

Wade didn't know if it was proper procedure to rush into surgery like that. He hadn't even signed the check-in clipboard. All he knew was that he was out of pain, a relief from the hours he'd spent suffering around others. He was hazy. And then he was out.

Δ

This night's pain and dread was much, much worse than his wisdom teeth were. Then, he knew that there might be some relief in his future, that you can extract a tooth or deaden a nerve. Though that night had him teary and screaming, it was temporary. Some end was in sight.

Dr. Emmett's body lying lifeless on his office floor, though, promised no end to pain and suffering for Wade. The dentist had made him feel safe and special, cared for and supported. But there was a price. His privacy. His secrecy. His family. His child. His freedom. Maybe his life.

"I'll take care of you," the doctor's words repeated, taking on different meanings as they echoed through Wade's rattled skull.

Δ

After his surgery two months before, Wade woke up in the backseat of his car, his shirt soaked in drool. The car was moving. He couldn't feel his own face. Someone else was driving, who? Who?

"Whoooooo are youuuu?" Wade tried to spit out. "Awwwahhhggh." Words would not come.

The driver was that black lady. That dental assistant. While driving, she was holding up her cell phone, taking some kind of selfie.

"Honey, keep talking," Celeste said. "You're hilarious."

"Whooo are youuuuu? Isss thiss really happening-ggg?"

"We're going to put this on YouTube," she said to him. "I'm driving you home. This shit is gold, baby."

"Whaaaat? WHOO ARE YOOOOOU?"

"Tell me again how pwetty my bwaids are, honey," Celeste said to Wade, eyeing him through the phone's camera. "Tell me again about how beautifuww dah dennis issss."

The nav system was guiding her to his house. How had she known the address? Wade dozed back off, unsure of anything, closing his eyes to the sunlight.

When he woke up again, he was in his basement bedroom. Jessa was there. The baby was there on the bed with him, poking his face. And, even though the whole day had just started for Wade, it was already night for everyone else.

"What gives?" he asked her, his mouth still tender.

"You've been out all day, Wade," her voice was more soothing than it had been that morning. "The dental nurse or whatever said you'd probably sleep 'til morning."

The baby cooed. And Wade zonked out again almost immediately.

Δ

It was that video, Wade thought now, his memory searching for the path that brought him to violence. That video revealed who he was and what he wanted. Celeste never posted it, but she must've shown it to the dentist. Because of it, Dr. Emmett caught him at his most vulnerable. Celeste thought it was just funny. And maybe she didn't know what kind of man Dr. Emmett was.

Dr. Emmett showed up at the grocery store three nights after the extraction, making sure Wade was his bagboy. When Wade pushed the cart toward Dr. Emmett's red Jeep, the conversation was more than polite.

"Your jaw hurt still?" the dentist asked.

"My appointment's in a couple days, sir," Wade said, touched by the man's concern. "I don't expect you to work on your time off."

"Don't be silly," Dr. Emmett said, his own smile sparkling. "Of course, I should ask."

"Well, I'm OK, I think," Wade admitted. They reached the Jeep. He stopped the cart. And Dr. Emmett took two steps toward Wade and grabbed his jaw deftly in his fingers.

"Open it," the dentist insisted.

Startled, Wade obliged and said "Ah," right there in the parking lot. Dr. Emmett stared for a moment, holding his face gently.

"Yeah," the dentist finally said smoothly. "I'd say you're OK." Their eyes met. It was charged.

And Wade closed his mouth.

Δ

After that, the dentist found his way to the grocery almost every day, always with bags to carry and with questions for Wade about his home life. And Wade appreciated the kindness. And Dr. Emmett kept leaving him with cash tips, even though Wade wasn't supposed to take them.

"Sir, I can't," Wade protested.

"It's Christmastime, kid," Dr. Emmett said. "And you have a baby at home." Wade shook his head.

"It's just between us," Dr. Emmett said to Wade while his eyes traveled the lean young man. "You think too much."

Δ

Come morning, Wade didn't know what might happen. He had to get the mouth out of his car. He had to know when the police found the body. He had to know if that guy Trevor would add it all up.

And then it occurred to Wade just how he could free himself from distractions to save his future. And, finally achieving some sort of solution, he finally was able to rest his eyes. Wade knew what he wanted.

Wade wanted his life out of Dr. Emmett's grip. He wanted a sense of control.

CHAPTER SIX

THE BABY AND THE ALARM BOTH STARTED BLARING AROUND THE SAME MOMENT AT 6 A.M., WAKING WADE FROM THE FOUR ROUGH HOURS OF SHUT-EYE THAT HE'D MANAGED TO GET. He headed to the toilet while Jessa grabbed Lydie out of her crib. To both girls, this was just morning routine. But Wade was charged with purpose. He had maybe three hours to set his life up on the right path before everything was ruined.

"Honey, why don't you get in the shower first?" he asked Jessa, who sat at the edge of the bed, preparing to turn on the news. "I can watch her."

Jessa glared at him, puzzled.

"What gives, Wade?" she asked. "You hate how long it takes me to shower. You complained about it literally yesterday."

"I overreacted," he said to her, heading toward the linen closet. Everything was only two steps away from everything else in the room, never meant to house anyone at all, let alone three people.

"I, um—," she started, shifting the baby on her lap. Then, she handed Lydie over to him. "This feels like a trap," she said to him.

"It's no trap," he said, winking and tossing her a blue towel with his spare hand.

"I don't know what this is about, but I'll take it," she said. And then she moved at her usual snail's pace toward the damn bathroom.

Wade watched as she shut the door, then waited for the sound of the shower. But there was nothing. Then, the toilet flushed. Then, nothing.

A full minute passed, and there was no sound at all. Wade tried to distract himself by changing Lydie's diaper. But, once that task was done and the baby was chill, he still couldn't hear any shower.

"Jessa, are you OK?"

"Yeah," she said.

"What happened to your shower?"

"Jesus, Wade," she snapped. "I'm looking at my damn phone."

"No big deal, baby," he said. "I was just checking on you."

At that, she turned on the tap. Water began flowing into the tub, then the shower spray resonated through the basement, and Wade got down to his most immediate business, heading out the door with Lydie in tow.

"We're going on a little adventure to the car," he sang to the baby as he rushed across the lawn barefoot in his T-shirt and boxer shorts, Lydie bouncing with each step. "Won't that be fun? Mommy takes such long showers, it gives us all the time we need."

Lydie squealed.

"I know, I knooooow," Wade said to her playfully. "We're being sneaky! Look at the driveway! Grandma's already gone to work!"

Mary's white Yaris was thankfully gone. Wade hit the unlock button on his key fob as he stepped off the lawn on to the driveway, tripping a little before recovering his balance. He did get startled, though, and that startled Lydie. Seeing the panic in his face before he could hide it, she started to wail.

Recovering his balance, Wade whispered quickly to his daughter, "It's OK. We're OK." But it was too late. Her lungs unleashed. Paranoid, he glanced at the neighbor's house, and he saw the blinds move. Wade nodded toward the window, letting them know that he had everything under control.

"Nothing to see, nothing to see," he whispered, bouncing her in his arms. Two seconds later, Lydie calmed down.

He continued toward the Prius, then opened the passenger door. Lydie started to struggle. "OK," he said to her as she persisted in wiggling. Wade opened the back door on the passenger side, then put Lydie into her car seat.

"We go bye byes."

At that, she giggled. Wade buckled her in, even though he hadn't intended to go anywhere, but he needed her to stay still while he did what was necessary. He closed the door on her, then returned his attention and his hands to his own passenger seat.

Wade grabbed the ceramic teeth, but he didn't know what to do with them right away. Unsure, he wrapped them in his shirt. He shut the car door, opened the window a bit, locked the car with his keys and headed back toward the house. It wasn't yet sunrise, and it was February in the suburbs of Atlanta. So, he figured Lydie could stay put while he put the mouth in his favorite hiding place. She'd be safe. He'd only be gone a sec. His mom had done this all the time when he was a kid, and she was a nurse. The doubt in his head began to whisper, but he'd been able to disregard that since everything went to hell yesterday.

When Wade was a kid, his favorite hiding place was the secret kitchen cabinet over the fridge. It was like his own personal cubby hole for random Little Debbies and Matchbox cars. It was one of those quirks of home construction, a storage area that was mostly out of reach that no adult ever used, not even for storage. Wade discovered it the way that boys discover most things, by climbing on things they shouldn't and sticking their hands in places without looking first. He figured he could claim the cabinet as his own when he reached in there at age 8 and had no fingers snapped off by a mousetrap or a rabid, crazed rodent. His mom never knew about it. She was always so tiny, never curious enough to climb her own kitchen.

Wade was lanky, flexible, and entirely too thin, no matter what he ate. Like his dad, he towered over everyone from around the time of middle school. It was no issue for him to climb up on the counter and sneak the teeth away until he could figure out what to do with them. He didn't want to throw them someplace where he'd never be able to get at them again. Better to know where they were.

It was no trouble getting to the kitchen, then putting the teeth on the counter. He noticed a hair caught in the braces and tried to wipe it away, but it was tangled in there. He didn't have time to address it, though, because he heard glass shatter and his child scream out in the driveway.

He rushed to the living room window to see what was happening, then saw the most bizarre sight. That neighbor lady, Mrs. Winston, was standing next to the car, holding an insanely freaked-out Lydie in her arms, brushing glass out of the baby's hair. At her feet was a claw hammer. She looked up into the window and glared at him. He looked back at the counter, where the mouth still waited for him to do something. Quickly, he rushed back to the kitchen, climbed the counter, grabbed the teeth and shoved them into the secret cabinet above the refrigerator. Then, just as quickly, he jumped off the counter.

Wade headed out the front door toward his Prius, which now had a busted backseat window, and toward Mrs. Winston, who looked mad as hell. He made his way around the glass, but he still managed to catch some in the soles of his feet.

"What did you do?" he asked her, wincing. "Get your hands off my daughter, you fucking bitch!"

"You left that baby in a locked car, you idiot jackass!" the neighbor screamed. "KIDS DIE LIKE THAT!"

"I was in the house a goddamn second," he screamed back. "I cracked the window! You should mind your own fucking business!" He reached for Lydie, who was screaming, but Mrs. Winston wouldn't give her over to him. "Give me my daughter! I swear to God!!!"

Wrapped in a towel, Jessa sprinted up the lawn toward the noise, barely managing to keep covered. She was screaming at them both, "What in God's name is going on out here???"

Mrs. Winston shouted, "I should call the cops on you for what you did to that baby!"

"Give me back my damn daughter, you stupid, fucking cunt!" Wade shouted, ready to punch Mrs. Winston. "Get the hell away from my house!"

Mrs. Winston bristled at the name calling, continuing to hold his baby away from him.

Jessa intervened, stepping between them and grabbing the baby in one arm and her towel in the other. But it didn't work. The towel dropped, which caused her to wail in frustration.

"Cut it out right now! Both of you!!" Jessa stepped delicately, trying to avoid the glass on the driveway, when she noticed the tool.

"Mrs. Winston, what are you doing with that hammer??"

Mrs. Winston's eyes blazed with fury.

"Your piece of shit boyfriend here locked the baby in the car and just left her to suffocate in the sun," she spat. "Don't either of you have any goddamn sense."

"More sense than to shatter a window in a baby's damn eyes, you fucking whore," Wade yelled at her. "I should call the cops on you. I was only gone in the house a damn second, for God's sake."

Mrs. Winston paused. "I don't care. You don't leave a kid in the backseat of a car unattended."

"You don't even have any kids," he cursed. "You should mind your own damn business."

"And neither of you should have kids," the lady said to them, glaring. "An idiot and a slut."

And Mrs. Winston grabbed her hammer and walked back toward her house.

"You're going to pay for this goddamn window," he announced as she retreated. Her reply to him was a hand gesture before she slammed the door to her house.

This day wasn't going to get any better than yesterday, Wade realized. Jessa stared at him.

"Did you really leave Lydie in a hot car while I took a shower?" she asked him, shaken with overdramatic concern for the baby.

He rolled his eyes.

"No, I did not leave her in a *hot* car," Wade ranted sarcastically. "It's February. Beyond that, I cracked a window before the sun came up and then went into the kitchen for one second."

"Why would you do that? Why not take the baby with you?" Jessa asked.

"I don't fucking know, Jess," Wade said, annoyed. "I just had to go to the kitchen."

Wade glared at her.

"And now I'm going back to the kitchen to get a broom and a trash bag for my car window. I can't fucking believe this."

He started to move away and then whined, "I guess you can drive her to daycare before school then while I take care of all this shit. Just put some fucking clothes on."

And Wade stomped off toward his mom's kitchen again.

Δ

During the drive to school, alone and tired, Wade tried listening to the audiobook in the Prius. He wanted a moment's calm. He wanted to feel normal and positive. He wanted to stop thinking about Jessa naked on the lawn with fury in her eyes. When was the last time that she wasn't even a little bit pissed at him? She barely knew anything about all the shit he was up to, yet Jessa's anger and disappointment always simmered at a low boil. He knew he deserved her anger. He knew he deserved more anger from her, in fact. But, for the longest time, he could not win with anyone, no matter what he did.

Lydie was a sweetheart, but babies—even good babies—try people's nerves. Jessa had this scowl she would aim at Wade at night, this look that screamed "You did this to me!" while she was doing homework or eating a Lean Cuisine while the baby cried.

When was the last time things were normal or even good between him and Jessa? He thought back before Lydie arrived around Christmas, which was just chaos.

The pregnancy had sucked, for the most part, for both of them. Once Jessa started to show, in particular, everyone in Waverly was a little bit like Mrs. Winston toward them, the judgmental stares, the fake Southern bullshit *"Bless your hearts."*

Wade wouldn't receive the looks as much as Jessa did. People knew who she was and who her daddy was.

So she started sending Wade out alone on errands. She wouldn't shop at his store anymore, just send him with a list of stuff to buy. They couldn't go to the movies or go to dinner even. Jessa said it was because they were supposed to save money, but Wade knew it was the good townsfolk that she was actually avoiding.

By the third trimester, Jessa was pretty much a shut-in, binging TV and eating junk food all day in his basement. In the most Southern way possible, Jessa had been "encouraged" to stay home from school that late in the pregnancy. The principal told her that her condition might "advertise" pregnancy to underclassmen, that the school didn't encourage "that kind of behavior," that the PTA might complain. After that meeting, Jessa didn't leave the house and barely left the glow of the television.

"He damn near called me the town whore," Jessa told Wade when he asked. Then, she got quiet. And stayed quiet. For hours.

Wade's mom raised an eyebrow toward Jessa on occasion in those days, though not out of annoyance. Mary told Wade that maybe the girl ought to talk to someone. But Jessa shrugged off any and all suggestions that she might be depressed. Instead, she would just blame her self-imposed exile on vanity.

"I'm as big as a house, Wade, hot and puffy all the time," she whined. "No way in Hell am I going anywhere."

Wade didn't argue with her, feeling too guilty that he had done this to her. She didn't need a fight in her condition. And Wade didn't tell her how he felt about the massive change their lives had seen, growing bigger inside

Jessa every day. Grown-ups get to act like a new baby is a blessed event. The only time Wade and Jessa celebrated the coming baby or felt blessed, instead of damned and cursed, was when they were at checkups.

Trips to the doctor were the only time Jessa would leave the basement that past October.

That was it, he realized.

The last time Wade felt normal, with Jessa or anybody, was the last ultrasound appointment, the one where the pictures looked more like a baby than a blob to him. The technician, who had always been super nice to them, introduced Wade and Jessa to their daughter's newest habits.

"She's growing bigger," the tech said warmly, getting excited. "She opens her eyes now. She's going to be so strong for y'all."

Wade was holding on to Jessa's hand. And he looked at her. And Jessa was smiling at their baby, who she knew was strong already because Jessa knew the girl was growing and kicking inside her. Jessa had read the baby books. She knew what to expect.

And, looking at his daughter, Wade started to sob. It hit him so suddenly, he jerked his body, and Jessa held his hand firm so that he couldn't break away.

"I just—I just don't want to fail her," he admitted to Jessa. "I'm scared I won't deserve her. Look how big she is. She's stronger than me already."

Jessa rubbed his arm tenderly.

"It's OK to be scared," the tech said to them both. "And it's OK to be excited."

Jessa added to this, "I think you're going to be a good dad."

"I don't know."

"I think all dads have that same worry," his girlfriend said. "My dad probably did. Your dad probably did."

Wade squeezed her hand. He was still crying a little, thinking about how his dad tried to pretend to be in a good mood for Wade's sake, no matter how sick he felt during the chemotherapy. He was a good father, right up to the end.

He whispered to her, "I miss my dad."

"It's OK," Jessa said. "I miss him too."

That was the day they chose the name Lydie, after his late father.

That was the last time Wade felt normal. The nightmare of the town whore in his basement and the baby that was going to ruin his entire future were more than just a series of mistakes. For that moment, they felt like a family to him.

Δ

Waverly High School was a safe, nice place where Wade could feel like the kid he actually was again. Throughout the tumult of the past few months, because Mary demanded he stay in school, he thankfully had moments where he didn't have to feel like a total, struggling adult.

Jessa had talked about maybe the two of them getting their GEDs so that they could work and make more money. But she just wanted out of his mom's basement. And her own family didn't want her around. Wade liked the chance to escape it all, even if it was for something as mind-numbing as a math class, but he had more to escape than Jessa did.

Because, for months, Wade concerned himself with Dr. Emmett in addition to everything else. Wade just wandered from disaster to disaster every day, except when he was in school.

Today, walking into Waverly just before the bell for first period, Wade knew that had to end, much as he dreaded it. To save himself and spare his family, he needed to be free to focus.

And it didn't take long for him to decide who he wanted to punch, at least. That part was the easiest.

That puny punk Victor Lennox's locker was four away from Wade's. Victor Lennox taunted Wade in gym class every day, calling Wade a fag, even after Jessa got pregnant and everybody knew it was a lie. Victor Lennox was an asshole. And Victor Lennox was standing next to his locker. And Victor Lennox looked at Wade and said hello.

So, Victor Lennox got his ass knocked to the ground. And then Wade crouched on top of Victor Lennox and kept punching him in his stupid face.

Thirty minutes later, Wade had a weeklong suspension from school. His mom had received a phone call. And Wade walked back to his car.

Instead of driving right home, like Mary ordered him to do, Wade drove directly toward the dentist's office, which—thanks to the weird office hours that Dr. Emmett kept—he knew was still a half hour from opening for business.

CHAPTER SEVEN

THE COST TO REPLACE A CAR WINDOW WAS AROUND $250. Wade's paycheck next Friday would be enough to cover it, but, until then, he was stuck choosing between a piece of cardboard and a Hefty bag to cover the backseat window. There was an advantage and a disadvantage to this, Wade thought. Covering the window, cleaning out the car and moving the baby seat from one side to another was something reasonable he could do right now in the dollar store parking lot while nonchalantly scoping out the dentist's office across the street, not drawing focus to himself. Still, having a covered back window meant that his blue Prius no longer blended in with the 3,000 other Toyotas on the road.

Armed with some duct tape and a collapsed Quilted Northern box, Wade prepared to make his car weather-resistant again, cursing Mrs. Winston with every moment of frustration. Lydie was never in danger with him. He was going to be right back. What kind of a person did Mrs. Winston think Wade was?

He glanced over at the dentist's office, waiting for Celeste to arrive, but there was still no sign of her. So, he patched more of the window.

With his week's suspension from school, maybe Wade could pick up some day shifts at the store. Repairing the car window wouldn't hit the family budget as hard. Maybe there'd be time to do all that, if the whole thing with Dr. Emmett wasn't solved by the cops immediately. Otherwise, Wade feared he'd have to be constantly on guard. Oh, who was he kidding? He was going to feel this anxious and scared for the rest of his life.

Money wasn't as much of a problem for his family, not as much as you'd expect. Wade worked all the shifts he could, and Jessa had a job answering phones at a used car lot on the weekends, mostly so that she could distract herself away from her old Sunday routine. And now that Dr. Emmett wasn't occupying his nights with "extracurricular projects," Wade thought that maybe he'd be able to do a better job around the grocery store.

The main reason that money wasn't tight, though, was because Wade's father wasn't alive. This was a tough thing for Wade and Mary to accept. Mary, in particular, never referred to the money they had as "Dad's life insurance." Instead, she called it by other names.

Once, right after Lydie was born, when she was a tiny, cute preemie in the NICU, his mom started to tease him in a way that seemed unfair.

"Well, kid," she said to him as they stared through the window. "There goes your college fund."

It stung. So, he stung back.

"I'm sure Dad doesn't mind spoiling the granddaughter he'll never get to meet."

At that, Mary excused herself to the bathroom, and Wade felt like a jackass the whole rest of the day, any time he looked at his mom. He let Mary hold the baby for an extra-long time that night, not even intervening when Jessa was sore, ready to nurse her.

Though his father had been gone four years at that point, he wasn't really a topic of conversation. Still, there wasn't an hour that passed where Wade didn't think about his father. Some stupid joke he made once, that weird floral cologne that he would wear when he was really dressed up and taking Mom somewhere—memories that would hit Wade funny, then like a train. In spite of himself, even now, he would cry about it. Lydie, if you held her in the light in just the right way, looked a little like his dad. But maybe that's just because Dad was bald too. And their eyes were the same.

Mary said Wade had his father's eyes, too, but he couldn't see it, no matter how often he looked for signs of it in the mirror. Wade couldn't see any of his father in his own face. His father certainly never acted like Wade had, not that Wade could tell.

His father would hate him for all the things Wade had done. Wade bounced from one disaster to another, thoughtlessly and selfishly. His father had been noble, certain, and decent to the end.

Wade was going to end up in prison for murder, a stupid, aimless loser kid who fucked and fucked 'til everything in his whole life was fucked. Everything was secrets, tricks and lies, and he never felt anything other than stupid.

Δ

In the beginning, Dr. Emmett would ask about how Wade was feeling, but sometimes it seemed like the dentist wasn't listening, just waiting for his turn to talk. Wade liked the talking, even more than anything else, but Dr. Emmett liked other things more. Dr. Emmett liked Wade's smile or the way Wade would get goosebumps when they would touch. The back of Wade's neck was really sensitive, and all Dr. Emmett had to do was breathe on him a certain way. The conversation would be over.

Δ

At the sight of Celeste getting out of her Oldsmobile with the faded paint job, the one that Dr. Emmett always said looked trashy, Wade snapped back into focus. The car window sealed, he returned to the driver's seat and watched the office, seeing what he could through the zoom lens on his phone's camera, which wasn't much. He didn't dare risk getting any closer, though.

She was bustling toward the door, four minutes late, eyeing Dr. Emmett's Jeep. Dr. Emmett used to bitch about Celeste's perpetual tardiness, how she always blamed it on her kids, even though the school day clearly started long, long before the dentist's office opened. Dr. Emmett used to say that she probably just talked everyone's ear off over sausage biscuits and those hash browns at Hardee's, where she went every damn morning. He said she'd probably go there until her inevitable heart attack.

"If you don't like her so much, why don't you fire her?" Wade would ask.

At that, Dr. Emmett would scoff and change the topics, as though it were something Wade would understand when he was older. Wade hated that kind of condescending adult shit.

Celeste would soon realize that she wouldn't need her keys to get in the door. The place was unlocked. Through his phone, Wade saw her shiver, certain that she was about to get blasted by her boss. Dr. Emmett said that she was always on eggshells around him, full of apologies and excuses, but she never actually fixed any of the behavior that irked him. She'd gossip too much. She'd be too friendly and forward with patients, which Wade knew firsthand. But Dr. Emmett said that she was smart and a problem solver, far cleverer than she seemed.

She disappeared into the office. Behind the blinds, Wade saw the lights of the office come on. He assumed she was already calling for the dentist, offering up her same old excuses. He saw her open the door to walk toward her desk. Then, he waited for Celeste to scream, assuming he'd be able to hear it even from across the street, through his broken back window.

But she didn't scream. Another moment passed; she didn't scream. And Wade, bracing for the thrill and the dread, instead felt confusion.

Like, surely, she saw the dentist's body slumped face down in front of the counter, that folder of papers scattered around him. Surely, she would shout and scream to try and revive him. And then Celeste would realize that the man was dead. It had been hours since Wade had bashed in his head. She would figure it out, and she would scream.

Instead, there was nothing. Nothing.

No sound. No noise.

Could Wade have dreamt the whole damn thing?

No. No, no, no. He had the teeth. He remembered how they thudded against the dentist's head.

And then, even weirder, someone else walked into the dentist's office, an old lady patient. Wade saw the lady walk up to the counter. And that lady did scream. But Wade couldn't see Celeste, he couldn't figure out what was even happening.

Δ

Five minutes passed, Wade frozen in anticipation and uncertainty, and then the police car showed up outside the dentist's office, blue lights and siren on alert. Wade took a breath at this sight, knowing that his troubles had officially begun.

But then something even stranger happened, and Wade couldn't look away from the scene. One moment after the cop showed up, then came a fire truck and an ambulance. All the crews rushed into the waiting room. Poor Wade didn't dare move. For some reason, even from a distance, he felt like everyone knew everything about him, that they were already coming to get him. Wade's life was already over. Quickly, the scene turned chaotic as crews rushed back and forth, and a set of paramedics went into the office with a stretcher and some equipment. People started to wander out of the other offices, gathering around the commotion.

And amid all that, to Wade's shock, the paramedics emerged from the office with Dr. Emmett on the stretcher, one of them squeezing a respirator. No one was doing chest compressions, though. He knew from Mary that someone would be doing chest compressions if there was no heartbeat.

Fear and hope took turns smacking Wade across the face and punching him in the gut, and he watched for the next telltale sign that his mom had warned him about.

"If the ambulance leaves its lights off, if it doesn't seem like it's in a hurry, then you know it's a lost cause," Mary had said to him once.

When the ambulance took away Dr. Emmett, though, its lights were flashing, and it sped toward the hospital like a bat out of hell. Celeste and that old lady watched from the sidewalk as it rushed away, veering around stopped traffic. Celeste began to pray, and the old lady patted her on the back in comfort.

Wade put the phone down away from his face. He began to cry, unsure of how to feel.

Wade knew less about what was happening than he had the day before.

Dr. Emmett was not a lost cause. At least, he wasn't yet.

CHAPTER EIGHT

WADE SUPPOSED IT SHOULD BE SOME KIND OF RELIEF TO DISCOVER HE WASN'T A MURDERER. But, as he sat again in his car waiting with so many questions and confusion, he wasn't sure where to aim all his anxiety. He had to direct his energy somewhere. But all the choices in front of him were dumb ones, and he couldn't afford to make any more mistakes. There must be some solution that would save his life.

Think of Lydie, he reminded himself. Think of Lydie and Mom. Everything he did from then on should be for them. Nothing else mattered. It wasn't about his comfort, his own loneliness, his own resentment about life. And his priority should never again be his own dick. Every stupid, selfish mistake he'd made in the past two months—all culminating in the whopper of a mistake yesterday—came about because Wade's priorities had been out of whack. Any moment where he'd thought dick-first about another person provided him with far more grief and guilt than pleasure. If he could manage it, Wade would never even think about sex again. But, man, Wade thought about it a lot.

Δ

Jessa wanted to lose her virginity, and Wade had been curious. So, they had sex a couple times, and she got pregnant. And then she got kicked out of her house, and—because she had nowhere to go with the baby and wouldn't fix the situation at a clinic or even talk about adoption—it was like he suddenly had a live-in wife and child when he was 16.

And some nights he'd get annoyed at Jessa for just being there in his space all the damn time, and he'd call Dr. Emmett to talk. Because Dr. Emmett was so understanding, friendly and willing to listen to him. And Wade didn't have any other guys at all he could talk to. He was outnumbered in his house by women, and they always managed to remind him of how he'd failed them all. He'd finish an UNO game on his phone, and he'd send a quick text to Dr. Emmett. He'd be on break at the store, and he'd send a message to Dr. Emmett. It got to the point where Dr. Emmett would show up at the store a half-hour before closing whenever Wade was working late. Dr. Emmett would buy two pints of ice cream, and they'd sit in the Prius and finish them off. And sometimes each other.

Wade thought Dr. Emmett actually cared, but that was a mistake. Dr. Emmett was an escape, a distraction, nothing to take seriously. Wade was a damned idiot for thinking it could be anything more than that. Dr. Emmett was 35, for fuck's sake. Dr. Emmett provided a break from everyday life, a quick and kinky secret that helped him get off. He closed his eyes and thought of Dr. Emmett some nights while with Jessa. Wade thought of Dr. Emmett some days during debate class, when he was buried in stupid research.

When life would get too noisy, Wade could think of Dr. Emmett, take matters into his own hand, get his stress under control, and force himself to relax. But it's a destructive impulse, a self-deception. He would disregard his own life and just jack his way through it. But it was no better than playing video games, a hobby he never quite saw the point of. Masturbation provided release, but, in the long run, it just wasted time and provided few solutions.

Δ

He sat in his car, tempted to go down to the dental office and grill Celeste about everything that had just happened. He thought about calling his mom at the hospital, where the ambulance had probably taken Dr. Emmett, and asking her for details about his condition. But both of those choices were exceedingly stupid. Like, there would be no reasonable explanation for how he already knew that the dentist was hurt. And, if the dentist was more than just hurt, if the dentist was DOA, Wade didn't want to hear about it and have yesterday's dread return.

He needed sleep. His mom had told him to go straight home from school after the suspension. Lydie was in daycare. He didn't have to go get her. And he just wanted to shut off his brain in any way that he could.

Wade's world was out of control. There was nothing he could do about it, except try to calm himself down, maybe get some sleep.

So, tacky and weird as he felt about doing this, Wade headed to the drugstore, the wind through the busted window making the whole ride noisy as heck. He walked toward the cold and flu medicine, grabbed himself some NyQuil. He couldn't buy sleeping pills; it would be too tempting to overdose. He didn't want to even tempt himself with that kind of escape. He just needed a nap. The clerk might card him if he got anything that could be used to make meth. Can they make meth with NyQuil?, he wondered. And then he went down the Family Planning aisle and grabbed a bottle of warming gel lube. A box of tissues. And some pens and a notebook. That way, the clerk wouldn't think he was a pervert.

Then Wade went home, went to his basement room, unloaded the bags, closed the blinds, took off his shirt, his pants, his underwear. He silenced his phone, plugging it into the charger.

He downed the shot of NyQuil like he'd seen people drink in the movies. He took the foil off the tip of the lube and peeled off the perforated cardboard from the Kleenex. And he laid down and attempted some slow breathing, some self-soothing. Trying to clear his mind of anyone he'd hurt, he thought about that delivery guy with the couch, whatever his name was. Trevor or something, his arms bulged when he lifted up that sofa.

The combination of efforts led Wade to doze off. So, sex wasn't completely useless.

Δ

Six hours later, when he woke up and looked at his phone again, Wade had five missed calls and four voicemails, which was weird because usually no one called him during a school day. Reviewing them, his stress level quickly returned. The first missed call was from a number he didn't recognize. Two were from Jessa. One was from his mother. And the last call looked like it was from Dr. Emmett.

CHAPTER NINE

TREVOR FORD ENJOYED HIS MORNINGS ALONE ON THE WAY TO WORK, THE ABILITY TO SING ALONG TO HIS PLAYLISTS AND DANCE WITH ABANDON IN HIS OWN DRIVER'S SEAT. Other drivers on the highway would stare at him as he bounced along to whatever song came up. He bounced even when a ballad came up. He could lip synch "Ode to Billie Joe" and, in fact, he did so frequently. The song made him laugh, even. Every day there was someone new who didn't understand him or care to connect with his vibe. Trevor didn't concern himself with them anymore, or he tried not to.

His moments of joy were hard-earned, and he was going to take them and appreciate them whenever they presented themselves. He was 20. He was healthy. He had a good job. He wasn't drinking anymore. He didn't live with his parents anymore. And yesterday, he'd met a cute, weird boy and gotten his number. And he'd gotten the boy to smile back at him.

When Whitney Houston came over the speakers to announce there was a boy she knew, the one she dreamed of, the lyrics connected with Trevor's spirit, and he made a promise to himself to acknowledge that a higher power—Whitney herself—was speaking to him and wanted him happy. She wanted him alive and silly and joyous.

Today, he vowed to call the boy. Today, Trevor would ask out that Wade, and their lives would start. And the weirdness would make sense.

Life was good. Life was romantic. Life was beautiful and epic. All you had to do was look for the colors, the light, the music, the humor. And it was all around. Trevor felt nice and cheery, for he was a guy named Ford driving a Chevy.

Δ

A couple months ago, Trevor had deleted his Facebook account, and that one small act had improved his mood so damn much that it surprised him. So, he deleted Instagram and Twitter too. And he only used YouTube for music. And not even new music. He used YouTube to find music that was at least a decade old, otherwise he wouldn't bother with it. Now, he filled his ears with songs that told stories and had messages. And none of the songs he found had a "(Feat. Blah Blah Blah)" credit on it. When Dolly Parton sang with Kenny Rogers, neither one of them was a guest on the track. They were both islands in the stream. That is what they were.

Things were almost immediately better. Like, he had no idea that it would be so much of a sea change in his attitude, but it was like night and day. He was even smiling sometimes. Trevor used to think it was a good practice for every person to be connected and informed about the news and their fellow man. But, nope, ignorance was bliss.

On top of not getting constant reminders of how his red-state home was failing him and intentionally screwing over people and causes that he held close to his heart, on top of not having to hear the President's name—except from those asshole Republican dip-shits at work that avoided him mostly anyway, Trevor found another benefit to avoiding social media. He no longer envied others as acutely. It made his brain less noisy. It was incredible.

Every morning like this was a gift, Trevor thought. It made every chore and struggle in his workday worth it.

He'd made the mistake of coming out to one of them during his first week there, assuming that people who worked with trendy furniture would be open-minded and culturally forward. But though the furniture was Norwegian, the drivers were red-state Americans.

Δ

By 9:30 a.m., when the manager had paired up all the drivers and crew for the day, Trevor knew that the entire workday would be something of a struggle. His partner was wearing a Confederate flag hat. Trevor's thoughts turned into words. In reply, there was a fist to his head right as the manager just happened to exit. And at 9:45 a.m., when Trevor was face down on the asphalt outside of Truck 22, with his entire crew standing over him and not one of them offering to help him up, his bright demeanor was a little dimmed. But only a little. He wouldn't let these bastards get him down. Another old song echoed through his head after he got knocked down, telling him to get back up again and never let them get him down.

He lifted himself first on to his elbows and knees, then staggered to his feet. Blood ran down his cheek like a slow drip from a leaky bathroom faucet. He smiled, huffing in and out to make sure he hadn't lost any teeth. Thankfully, he hadn't. So, Trevor raised his head in the direction of the dude who'd knocked him down, keeping the smile plastered across it. A crowd was gathered around them, none of them cheering for Trevor.

"So that's a 'no' from Mike," he said cheerily, acknowledging the man behind the fists who was supposed to be his partner today.

"Does no one else want to ride shotgun with me on deliveries today?" Trevor asked the men.

Trevor was resolute, so they walked away, back to their assigned rides. He went to the bathroom to clean up the blood. He'd be alone again today. Yesterday, he was paired with Julio, a reluctant, quiet guy who would ride with him for a while and then abandon him midshift, which is how he met Wade, so Trevor couldn't be all mad.

Today, his manager would probably assign him to move boxes around the warehouse, just to give him something to do and to avoid the tensions.

Trevor appreciated the opportunity to stay in the comfortable warehouse. And he hoped—for one second, before his positivity returned—that Mike would have a heart attack and die.

Δ

Trevor had no recourse about the harassment. No one had expected him to stay in this job, not even him. The mean ones treated him like he was a faggot. The nice ones acted like he was a kid on a gap year regarding them the way an anthropologist studies a strange tribe. Since Trevor worked like a man biding his time, no one wanted to treat him like he belonged. Trevor didn't belong there.

He had expected this job to be more tolerant and open-minded, since the furniture company prided itself on open-minded Norwegian values and pronunciations, but the delivery guys were rather alpha and tribal and didn't take to him at all. Trevor wanted shiny, happy people instead of these belligerent dolts from hell.

"I wish this was Norway," Trevor said to himself in the bathroom mirror.

Then he smiled and realized aloud, "Oh well, you're still pretty, from the soul on up."

Trevor was pretty. It used to get him into trouble, all kinds of kinky, illegal trouble that you find when you don't want to go home to your parents but don't have anywhere else to go. But those days were gone. He had a better life now, even if it still meant that people were going to bloody his face a little.

He put on his earbuds and went about shuffling furniture on to other delivery men's trucks, paying the men themselves no mind at all.

At 11:30 a.m., on his lunch break, Trevor placed the call to Wade, even though he didn't know what to say. He couldn't very well tell the kid that there was no delivery partner last night, that Trevor had texted himself just so that he could keep Wade's number. He couldn't think of any way of admitting that wherein he wouldn't sound completely nuts. So, Trevor didn't leave the boy a message.

He did listen to the kid's outgoing message, though, just to hear the boy's lovely tenor voice again.

"Hi, this is Wade Harrell! Leave a message after the beep."

It was a lovely voice. But such an odd name. And so weird. Trevor hung up before the beep.

Wait, the delivery last night went to Dr. Emmett's office. What kind of son doesn't have his father's last name? It was possible, of course, but it still struck Trevor as puzzling. He'd have to ask Wade about it whenever they had their date. And they would have a date, Trevor assured himself. The world was beautiful. Things were working out for Trevor from now on. It was destined. It was fate. Today was a good day.

CHAPTER TEN

AFTER A MOMENT'S HESITATION THAT THE DOORS OF SALVATION BAP-
TIST CHURCH WOULD BE BARRED TO HER, LIKE HER PARENTS HAD
WARNED, JESSA LANCASTER FOUND THAT IT WAS EASY TO JUST BURST
RIGHT THROUGH THEM ON A WEEKDAY MORNING, STROLLER IN TOW.
Her father was going to meet his grandchild. He was going to meet his grandchild right now, Jessa vowed. She
saw his car in the parking lot while she was taking the
baby to daycare, and, after considering it for a half hour
while she circled the block and the baby rested, Jessa decided to just visit the dear reverend. If he wasn't going to
return her calls or reply to her emails or ignore her at the
store, now he could look her and her damn baby in the
face and not talk. It was time to end all this nonsense. She
could no longer wait for the adults in her life to be adult.
Her life was not some damn Lifetime movie.

Jessa hurried down the long stretch of crimson carpet toward his office, the same hallways she and her sister Traci would run down at least once a week when she
was growing up, pretending to be movie stars waving
to fans. This section still smelled of old books and grape
juice, and she had to keep rushing before she became
intimidated by how important she'd always been taught
this place was. She had to get to her father's office before
God stopped her. She had to see her father before she
was too nervous to knock on his door, interrupting his

important work. Jessa needed her father to be an understanding man, not a figure on a pedestal that she was too scared to talk to. Other people were able to come to him with their troubles, and she envied them as a girl. Jessa needed her father's counsel and help.

Doors here were supposed to be open to those seeking help, Jessa thought as she wheeled Lydie even further down the long, long hallway. Jessa didn't know if Lydie was awake or asleep, her sole focus was on getting this done, getting the stroller through the door of his office. His actual office, too. Not just the reception area where Virginia Dean, the church secretary, sat. Lydie Harrell was going to meet her grandfather today, by God.

Jessa got to the heavy oak door, the one set off from the main hallway by a little vestibule—even a side prayer room. It was intended to be majestic and intimidating. Jessa turned the stroller with both hands so that it trailed behind her, and she kicked the door open with all her might and momentum.

Jessa was raised to be a good girl and an example. She was in pageants from the time she was a toddler, and her smile lit up rooms. Good girls don't raise their voices, except in choir or onstage when a spotlight complements their star qualities and highlights their beauty. Good girls behave themselves, never interject in conversations or insist upon the attention of men. She was always asked by men, "And, how are you?" Never just "How are you?" The "And, how are you?" came after she inquired about their well-being first and the men went on for five minutes without stopping. Men never wait to be asked.

She was done waiting to be asked for anything. She had given her father months to come around on his own. The kick rang out as a blast through Virginia's waiting room, causing the secretary to shiver. Virginia was a pious and catty old gossip. Jessa knew this. Jessa also guessed that her pregnancy and excommunication had been a favorite topic of the old lady's these past months. Virginia deserved a shock.

"What on Earth?" Virginia squealed.

"I took three years of ballet, Mrs. Dean," Jessa said. "Of course, I can kick."

"Jessa, what are you even doing?" the lady asked, even though she saw the damn stroller and was not an idiot.

Jessa wheeled it past the lady, who got up out of her chair and tried to block the door to dear old Rev. Lancaster's office.

"Don't even, Mrs. Dean."

"You can't just barge in here, young lady. I know for a fact that he doesn't want to see you."

"I can kick through you just as easily as I can kick through the door, Mrs. Dean," Jessa said coldly. "Don't make me prove it."

Virginia scoffed.

"Don't act appalled," Jessa said. "Just open the door. This isn't a discussion."

"No, I can't do that," Virginia said. "You aren't welcome here."

"God says everyone is."

Another voice echoed from the opposite side of the door.

"I don't want to see you, Jessa," the reverend said to his daughter.

The boom in his voice contained no warmth. She saw only the outline of his silhouette through the stained-glass window on the door. He was so cold.

"Go to school, Jessa," he said. "Go anywhere. Just go away."

It took her a moment to compose herself. For some reason, she thought she'd get the first word. Having no plan of attack was a terrible plan of attack, she realized.

"I have the baby with me, Daddy," she said, trying not to falter in voice or mission. "See my baby."

"Go."

"Her name is Lydie, Daddy. Lydia Ruth Harrell. First name came from Wade's dad. I provided the middle one, after Mom's mom. Does Mom know that already? Did anyone tell her? I don't know what you know."

Virginia glared at the baby. Lydie just giggled at her. And Virginia, in spite of herself, cracked up at the baby. The old lady wasn't made of stone. And it's harder to hate something when it's in front of you, being cute and giggly.

Jessa kept talking at the door, waiting for the other glacier to melt.

"She looks like you, Daddy. And not just because every baby looks like a shriveled old bald man. She has your nose and your ears. I used to think that people were stupid for saying stuff like that, but, seriously, when she gets irritated, she looks like you do."

She paused.

"I wish I didn't know your irritated face so well, Daddy," Jessa confessed.

"Jessica, please," her father said through the door. "I've made my feelings about this incredibly clear. You made choices that I cannot support."

"I think you're scared of my baby," Jessa said.

"What?" he asked, appalled.

"I think you know you're wrong and that you'll love my baby once you see her," she said, bold as ever. "I don't think that this is about teaching me shame or regret. I don't think this is about punishing me. I think this is about you."

At that, he cracked open the door and eyed her through the space. Only her. He wouldn't look at the baby.

"Go away, Jessica."

"No. Come out."

He shut the door again.

"What's so scary about a baby, Daddy? The idea that you might like something that came out of my disobedience?"

"You didn't just disobey me, little girl."

Emboldened, Virginia lifted Lydie out of her stroller and began to cradle her. Virginia even started humming to the girl.

Jessa said, "God can judge me, Daddy. You don't need to do it for Him. Heck, I even judge myself for it enough. You don't need to keep doing this. Let me come home."

"I thought so," Rev. Lancaster said. "I knew you weren't just here to show me the baby." At that, he opened the door and looked her in the face. Rev. Lancaster turned, nodded at Virginia and then put his arms out to hold the baby. It wasn't a moment as warm as Jessa would've wanted. In her imagination, he would have cried and professed his love for Lydie and Jessa, all at once.

He just put Lydie in the stroller, regarding her for a moment.

"She's cute, I'll give you that," he told his daughter, securing his grandbaby in her seat. "But you can't bring her into my house."

Then, Rev. Lancaster nodded back toward the hallway and said he'd walk them out. Jessa felt like she'd been kicked as hard as she kicked the door.

They exited the church office together, Jessa pushing the stroller. She tried to feel proud that he'd finally met his granddaughter, but it wasn't all that she wanted.

The hallway seemed just as long on the way out. She wasn't even sure if she was allowed to say anything else. Her father was dismissing her from church like they were in the father-daughter confrontation scene from "Dirty Dancing." Jessa had to do something.

"Will you tell Mom that you saw me?"

"Sure, Jessa," he said to her.

"I really do want to come home, Daddy."

"That can't happen."

"Daddy," she said, her voice breaking for a moment. "I'm sorry I came here. It's just—"

"What now, Jessa?" His tone was suspicious. Rev. Lancaster knew his daughter. He'd been wrapped around her finger before, but he thought he knew better than to fall for it again.

She took a quick breath.

"Wade *hurts* me, Daddy. And today he tried to hurt my baby."

CHAPTER ELEVEN

JESSA PULLED A BLANKET OUT OF THE STROLLER AND PLACED IT ON A PATCH OF LOOSE PINE BARK ON THE CHURCH LAWN, THINKING LYDIE COULD USE SOME "TUMMY TIME" LIKE SHE RECEIVED THESE DAYS AT DAYCARE. Her father was holding the baby while Jessa arranged everything.

"We used to do the same thing with you on this very lawn," Rev. Lancaster said to her. He didn't coo at the baby, didn't say little things in the squeaky voice he reserved for babies from the congregation. Jessa knew her father delighted in children, for she'd seen him with Sunday Schoolers and in the nursery. Heck, she remembered how he fussed over her and her sister when they were little. Lydie was receiving no affection from him, and she was squirming and screaming. Rev. Lancaster didn't do anything to calm her down.

So Jessa scooped up her baby from his arms, and Lydie stopped fussing. Jessa felt victoriously maternal. She turned to her father and smiled.

He was frowning over how she held Lydie.

"Don't ever do that," Rev. Lancaster said to his daughter. "If you pick her up every time she cries, she'll figure it out and use it against you forever."

Jessa hesitated, assuming her father probably knew more about parenting than she did. But she couldn't give him the satisfaction. She placed the baby on the blanket on her tummy, watching as her chubby little arms couldn't even lift herself up. Soon, the baby dozed off.

"Just keep talking to me about what happened with that Wade," Rev. Lancaster told her.

"I don't know, Dad," Jessa tried to explain. "It's like he's checked out most of the time, finding excuses to not come home—or he's yelling at me. And, this morning, he locked the baby in his car and went in his mom's house."

"He used you for what he wanted, and now he can't face up to the consequences of it."

"It's not like that, exactly," she replied. "He wasn't the one who wanted—"

"You were manipulated, Jessa," Rev. Lancaster said. "Wade ruined you, telling you he'd be there for you, and now it's all too real for him."

"Maybe that's some part of how he feels, Daddy. He didn't promise me anything, but he's provided more for me lately than you or Mom have. Also, Wade didn't ruin me. Girls can't get ruined any more than boys can."

"Show me any good man who would take you on now," Rev. Lancaster said, waving toward the baby. "With that kind of baggage."

"Baggage?" Jessa asked, insulted for her baby's sake.

"You know what I mean," he scoffed.

"Yes, but I'm tempted to have you say it out loud so that you can hear yourself."

"Does he physically hurt you, Jessica?" her father asked, a bit eager for more reason to hate Wade. He had known Wade from around town for years, but now, betrayed, he talked about the boy like he was a total stranger.

"Not so far," Jessa said, carefully selecting her words. "But Wade does have a temper. Sometimes I worry he's just going to blow up at someone someday."

"I'm scared for you, dear," her father said.

"Then let me come home."

Δ

Five minutes later, as her father watched and her baby slept, Jessa called Wade's cell. It went to voicemail.

"Wade, call me when you get this," Jessa said. "When you get out of class or whatever. Just call me soon. It's important."

Her father scowled.

"Of course, that little shit didn't answer," he said.

"Daddy, you're still at work," Jessa said to him. "Someone from inside might hear you."

Rev. Lancaster shrugged.

"They'd be more scandalized by you and the baby than they would be by hearing me say four-letter words."

"Really, Daddy?" Jessa said. "I know for a fact that some of the babies in the daycare here are just as 'scandalous' as I've been."

"You're my daughter, though," Rev. Lancaster asserted.

"I'm a preacher's kid, behaving the way preacher's kids always have," Jessa said. "It's so cliché they write songs about it, Daddy."

He laughed.

The tension had lightened between them, all it took was one heart-to-heart and a couple exaggerations about

Wade being dangerous. And it had been decided. She could come home, bringing the baby with her, by the end of this week. All Rev. Lancaster had to do was clear it with Jessa's mom, which wouldn't take much convincing. Apparently, Mrs. Lancaster had been crying randomly for two months, all through Christmas and then sporadically since. There were days when the woman wouldn't get out of bed, Rev. Lancaster said. They could give living under one roof again a try, he said. You and the baby, he said. He wouldn't call Lydie by her name. That would change in time, Jessa hoped.

Δ

Wade and Mary's house had been a nice house, and Mary in particular was so sweet with the baby. Wade was sweet and loving, too, but Mary was a seasoned mom and a seasoned nurse. She knew what to do. She was nurturing. Wade fumbled and tried and loved Lydie. But he didn't love Jessa, and Jessa could feel it. Since she moved in, they'd been like roommates instead of lovers. They fought too easily. Jessa felt like she was intruding whenever she walked into their kitchen. She was like a houseguest who stayed long past her welcome, and she wanted to go home.

This would not be an easy transition or an easy break-up. But it was better to do it now before the baby got used to this situation, Jessa thought. She wanted her own family back. She wanted her baby to have the people that she grew up with loving her the way they'd loved Jessa.

Her mom had made her a pageant girl, taught her manners and how to be agreeable. Jessa and Traci were always in the prettiest dresses their mom could find. They were a model church family.

Now, though, they'd be a modern church family. And maybe the Baptists would like that, Jessa prayed, knowing she was lying to herself.

"We'll figure this out, baby," Rev. Lancaster said to his daughter. "I don't want you around that horrible boy anymore."

Jessa looked in her father's eyes, noting the anger behind them. It wasn't just toward Wade. She knew he was still mad at her, too, and that he'd make her pay for it once she got home. But she still wanted to be home.

Suddenly, from the lawn, Lydie erupted in screams and tears, twisting on her stomach, a weird, urgent tone that immediately alarmed her mother. Like nothing, Jessa grabbed her girl.

Her father remained seated.

"What is it?" Jessa asked, trying to keep her voice neutral and sing-songy. "What is it, honey?"

The cries continued to echo weirdly, as though Lydie didn't have the breath for them. The baby trembled, continuing to scream.

And a wasp flew off the baby's leg, a sight Jessa noticed from the corner of her eye as a blur.

"Daddy, what's wrong with her? She's changing color."

"I, uhhh—" her father said, finally rising from his seat.

"Daddy, please! I think she got stung!"

He grabbed his daughter by the arm, led her to his SUV.

"Is she allergic?" he asked frantically as they rushed through the hallway, into the parking lot to his reserved space.

"What about the car seat?" Jessa asked, holding her baby tight. Her tears were coming fast. "We need her car seat!"

"Just hold her," her father ordered. "We're going to the emergency room."

Lydie wailed in her mother's arms as her grandfather sped them down the road, her body tense and burning with pain.

Δ

Ten minutes later, as they sat in Triage and waited for a doctor, Jessa called Wade again, the baby screaming in her arms. His phone still off, she delivered a second voicemail.

"Come to your mom's hospital when you get this!" she shouted. "We're in the emergency room. Something's wrong with Lydie."

Rev. Lancaster closed his eyes and prayed, afraid to look at the baby. He didn't want to be scared for this baby. He didn't want to care about it. He didn't want to love her. God wasn't playing fair.

For months, he had wished that his daughter hadn't been disgraced or caused him shame. He wished he hadn't been so mad at her. He wished she hadn't turned his home life into utter chaos, rendering his wife practically immobile with sorrow and disappointment.

Now, after only a morning where he momentarily allowed his resolve to weaken long enough for one conversation, Rev. Lancaster prayed that his baby granddaughter wouldn't die before he got to know her.

Lydie continued to cry, growing weaker from the effort and turning red and splotchy from the sting.

Jessa looked from doctor to doctor, hoping that anyone might be the person sent to examine Lydie. She texted Mary to let her know that they were there and that she should come downstairs as soon as she could.

"Daddy, why is this taking so long?" Jessa pleaded with her father.

Rev. Lancaster glanced around the room, stopping the first person in scrubs he could find.

"Sir, I think my granddaughter is having an allergic reaction," the reverend pleaded.

"Sorry, sir, it'll be just a moment," the doctor said. "Ambulance just brought in a guy with his skull cracked open."

CHAPTER TWELVE

IN THE MIDDLE OF THINGS, AFTER THE TALKING HAD PROGRESSED, AFTER DR. EMMETT HAD WORKED HIS WAYS AROUND THE INITIAL WALLS OF WADE'S CONFUSION AND RELUCTANCE, AFTER DR. EMMETT TUGGED AWAY AT WADE TO RELIEVE HIS STRESS, AFTER WADE HAD BECOME WILLING ENOUGH TO TRY SOME ORAL STUFF, THE TWO CONSPIRATORS HAD CONTRIVED A WAY TO SPEND THE NIGHT TOGETHER. It was a January weekend night, and the high school basketball team was playing in a state tournament out of town. Wade told his mom and Jessa that he wanted to go support his friends. And they were so preoccupied with all the new baby stuff, at which they had probably realized he was useless, that they kind of shrugged off his requests to go with little complaint, so long as it was only for a night. Dr. Emmett was thrilled, eager to show Wade a full range of experiences. Wade was nervous with a tension that he carried from his shoulders to his toes and all stops in between. He wanted to please Dr. Emmett, but he didn't know quite how to be, well, gay. Or bi. Homosexual. Heteroflexible. Open. Slutty. Or whatever it was that he was.

Wade didn't feel like his sexual desires entirely fit what other people needed him to want.

His dick was amenable enough to any sort of stimuli, but most of the time he felt like he was checked out of his body. Like, things were happening, but he wasn't there. He was elsewhere as his own cock crowed. If Dr. Emmett wanted to suck him off, then the soldier stood at attention. If Jessa read something in a Harlequin romance that she wanted to try, his soldier would oblige with a salute. But Wade himself couldn't figure out which side his soldier preferred. His dick was a draftee, shooting wherever he was told to aim.

Wade was 16. He wasn't supposed to know what he wanted. But the fact that he didn't never ceased to bug the hell out of him. Wade wanted to be decisive. He wanted to be faithful. He wanted to be honest and good. And he wanted to know what he was supposed to like because, if biology was any indication, he liked everything. And it unnerved him.

The first time he and Jessa did it, Wade was aroused. His penis functioned. He was able to perform or whatever. She mounted up on him while they watched Marlene Dietrich, which was weird enough, and Jessa kept guiding his hands toward her bra. She unfastened it after he couldn't get the damn thing undone. And it fell from her shoulders to her elbows and just caught there. And her breasts were exposed, and it was the first time Wade had ever seen breasts in person. And the whole thing went from surreal to real, and it was exciting and surprising at first. Jessa's boobs weren't massive. They were cute, and Wade tried to touch them the way he'd seen people do it in the movies. But it just felt like he wasn't doing it right. He just kept pawing at them, swiping at them, like he was a kitten trapped under two balls of yarn. Eventually, he just cupped them and asked her if that was OK. And Jessa moaned a bit. But it felt like they were just playing at sex, imitating scenes from movies, guessing what to do next.

Dr. Emmett's body was a map that was easier for Wade to read. He had a better sense of what to do with the dentist because they had the same equipment. There was no learning curve, at least not in the stuff they'd done so far. Wade worried, though, about the raised stakes. Things were moving too fast. The hotel room might be a game changer. He'd never touched those areas of himself, afraid of what it might make him. Worse, it might hurt.

"I'm going to see Nelson play point guard, it's just double-A, but I think they have a shot," he said to his mother, who wasn't really listening. She was holding the baby, regarding Lydie with this sort of awestruck face, an unconditional love incapable of ever disappointing her or letting her down. Wade didn't know what a point guard was supposed to do exactly. Guard, he supposed. He kind of knew Nelson from elementary school, and he'd read on some locker decoration that he was a point guard. He wanted authentic details so that no one would suspect that he wasn't telling the entire truth. But no one asked him.

Wade felt certain about nothing, except that he was some loser failure who couldn't do anything right. That he was certain about. That is how he felt all the time. And doing things to try and help people or satisfy people provided him with no relief or answers.

"What's up with you lately?" Jessa asked him while he was packing. "You seem so—"

"What? Sad?" Wade asked her, a defensive tone in his voice.

"Different," she answered.

The days of Tic-Tac-Toe were done. He couldn't really talk to her anymore about his struggles. She wasn't detached from his problems. She was there in them, adding to them, confusing them, all the time without knowing she was doing it. She meant no harm at all.

Δ

Wade tried to remember happiness, a freedom from worry. He thought about fishing with his dad and how boring it was. Even now, missing his father as much as he did, Wade still couldn't romanticize fishing trips. Fishing trips at Lake Waverly were quiet and dreadfully boring. And Wade always thought it was pointless that, in the off chance that either he or his dad would catch a fish, neither of them would keep the thing. They would throw it back every time.

"I can't bring that back to Mary," his father would tell him. "She wouldn't want to clean it."

Wade's memories of his dad were never satisfying enough. He thought of conversations he wished he could have or things that he'd wished he'd said. Wade wanted his dad to be the one with all the answers, but he couldn't romanticize their time together. There was never a moment where Wade felt perfectly all right. There was never an answer that was absolute, something that would provide the boy with a map on how to be a good person.

Instead, his father would answer him in iffy statements or wouldn't understand the question. And Wade just got the sense that adults had no definite answers either.

Δ

As he drove to meet Dr. Emmett in the parking lot of the dental office on that January night, Wade actually prayed to his father for guidance.

"Dad, I don't think I love Jessa," he prayed. "I love Lydie. But I don't love Jessa. I don't mean to get so mad at her, and I don't mean to cheat on her. And she's a cool girl who doesn't really deserve this. But I don't know what to do."

"Son, you keep making these choices. Jessa isn't the only one making the choices. You aren't blameless."

What came next didn't feel like an answered prayer, it just felt like an imagined talk. An answered prayer would feel different, Wade thought. An answered prayer would feel like it contained some certainty.

"Wade, do you think you love this dentist? Who is he, even?" he imagined his father asking.

"Dr. Emmett likes me," Wade answered his dad. "He shows up at the store every night. He talks to me. He listens to me."

"But what are you even saying to him?"

"Mostly, I think I talk to him about you," Wade said to his father, who was only in his head and wasn't actually there to be of any help or offer him any hugs or anything. "Or I talk to Dr. Emmett like I would talk to you. But it isn't just that. I mean, it feels good to be liked like that, touched like that. I don't know."

"He isn't me, Wade," he imagined his dad telling him. He imagined his dad spoke to him in a soft, calm voice. He missed that voice. His dad never used it enough when he was alive. It was reassuring, loving and safe.

"Seriously, it isn't just that. What if I'm—?"

"Wade, it's OK to not know who you are," his imaginary dad said in just the right way. "It's the same with everybody."

But Wade was fairly certain that wasn't true. Some people knew exactly who they were. He didn't understand why he couldn't be one of those people. It would be so much simpler.

By the time Wade arrived in the parking lot, landing his blue Prius in its usual spot, the teen was crying. He wiped his tears and waited for the red Jeep to meet him. They were going to a Days Inn. Dr. Emmett said they could pretend to be father and son.

Δ

Hours later, Wade stood in front of one of the double beds, shirtless in his boxers, waiting for Dr. Emmett to emerge from the hotel bathroom. He wasn't sure if he needed to be standing or sitting when the dentist opened the door after his shower. None of their previous encounters, always in a car, had been this planned. So, Wade was trembling, a mix of nerves and a really powerful heating unit that fogged the windows. This night, things were going to happen, thorough things. And no amount of porn Wade watched—in secret, in his car, when no one could catch him—could prepare him. Every move looked like it kind of hurt. Some of the activity looked like it might be worth the hurt, at least according to some of the participants onscreen.

But those dudes were professionals. And, like, acrobats.

Wade was curious about some of the stuff, some of the videos aroused him—the complicated ones with stories and seductions, and he trusted Dr. Emmett not to push him too far. And Wade kept looking at the two beds, knowing that he could always retreat if things got too painful, without having to sleep on the floor.

Still, they hadn't really talked about it. Most of the ride up, Dr. Emmett asked him just stuff about the baby and how school was going. About 45 minutes in, Wade just went into this long rant about how much of a bitch the grocery store manager was about Wade requesting this time off. Dr. Emmett just chuckled at him, seeming to only be half-listening. Dr. Emmett spoke of nothing from his own life, except to say that Celeste was doing fine and keeping the office a funny place to be. To cut through the silence and to stop conversation from turning more invasively personal, Dr. Emmett put the radio on the oldies station, introducing Wade to pop music from the Eighties and Nineties.

After one particularly silly song by someone named Martika that Dr. Emmett knew every word to, some sing-songy one that sounded like a playground chant, Wade broke the tension that only he seemed to be feeling.

"So is your name Maxwell or, like, Maximilian?"

"What?"

"Your name, Dr. Emmett," Wade clarified. "What is Max short for? The sign outside your office just says Max Emmett, DDS."

Dr. Emmett winced, then tried to recover his composure.

"Wade, you can just call me Dr. Emmett if it's easier for you. It'd be weird if you called me Max."

"Sorry," Wade muttered, unsure what he'd done wrong. They'd blown each other for weeks. Dr. Emmett had been inside his mouth with a variety of tools and methods. A first-name basis didn't seem uncalled for.

"It's OK, kid."

Δ

All of this echoed in Wade's head, making him feel like the world's most stupid idiot, as he continued to question whether to sit or stand in front of the bed or whether he should remove his own boxers. He wondered if he'd be allowed to ask questions. He wondered what his mom would think if she could see him right now. He wondered if Dr. Emmett had lied about STDs or HIV or stuff. What if Dr. Emmett tried to kiss him? Had the wine Dr. Emmett given him before the shower been roofied? Why had they never kissed before? What even was this? Like, if Dr. Emmett was a serial killer, then Wade was just minutes away from getting strangled or something, and maybe this was all a trick. This was all unsafe. It was all a mistake. It was all a terrible idea, and he was going to ruin his life. And what if he was bad at it? Would Dr. Emmett laugh at him?

The bathroom door opened. Dr. Emmett, short, muscled and a little furry across his chest, wafted into the room amid a cloud of steam and Old Spice body wash, wrapped in a towel. He paused, regarding Wade's body. Dr. Emmett had these penetrating green eyes. His smile was sly. Wade felt his gaze, and its effect prickled across his shoulders like static. Wade's ardor betrayed him, the boxers suddenly alert.

Dr. Emmett moved closer. Dr. Emmett whispered hello to Wade, the words directed toward his neck and his shoulder blades. And then, warm and charged, Dr. Emmett wrapped his arms around him, tenderly and safely. And Wade still kept shivering.

"It's OK," Dr. Emmett said to Wade's ear, biting the left lobe, exhaling over it, pulsating with heat. "You don't need to worry about anything tonight. Just relax. There are no mistakes. I just want you to enjoy yourself."

Jessa was never like this. Dr. Emmett's body was firm, certain. He held Wade still. He said he wanted to focus on Wade. Jessa was never like this, for she was full of questions, nerves, and worry herself.

They just held each other in an embrace, Dr. Emmett's mouth probing Wade's neck, Wade's ears, Wade's chest.

And then it happened. Wade tilted his head to moan, and Dr. Emmett kissed him. Softly, only lips grazing at first. Then, they lingered. Tips of tongues touched, indicating intent, the give-and-take of a dance. Wade lowered his own boxers. Dr. Emmett's towel fell. His whispers continued, making offers, positions, guidance. Dr. Emmett was never demanding, Wade's curiosity was allowed to dictate the direction that things went. Warm. Tender. Good. New. For hours.

Dr. Emmett turned the television on low volume so that no one would hear them and suspect anything. A cable channel was showing all the "Leprechaun" movies, and they just kept going. Every once in a while, Wade would glance from his lover to the flickering screen, watching the green-suited mini-monster stalk some blonde and demand his stolen gold. And Wade would giggle, which made Dr. Emmett just work harder to keep Wade's attention.

Neither of them talked of feelings or meaning. There weren't many words at all once they found themselves on the same page, traveling the same road. But Wade had never felt anything so intense before. For hours, there was no one else but the two of them.

That night, he loved the dentist. And the dentist's body had never looked so excited.

Δ

As Dr. Emmett lie unconscious in a hospital bed a month later as surgeons tried to save him, as Wade sedated himself with NyQuil to escape from the stress and the pain all afternoon, that Days Inn night—their only night where they did everything and didn't worry about hiding or schedules—played a highlight reel across both of their memories, giving neither of them easy conclusions. Is a situation entirely tragic if you enjoy some part of it? Are you a victim if you actively participate in your own corruption? Neither of them could answer these questions with certainty. When you know you're dreaming, you wake up. That crazy February afternoon of head injuries and bee stings, neither of them did.

CHAPTER THIRTEEN

A DENTIST'S OFFICE IS NEVER A PLEASANT PLACE TO SPEND TIME. Its main duties are to scrape, pull, or drill at your face. Patients are either terrified about an appointment or annoyed and filled with dread about it. Either way, ain't nobody terribly polite about being there. Celeste Parker knew this, and she brought low expectations for a "good day" to work with her every morning. She also brought with her the same snide, dry sense of humor that had gotten her through every day of her life. Dr. Emmett warned her repeatedly that one day her attitude would get her into trouble.

Usually she just arched an eyebrow at him. But yesterday, on her way out the door to get her son instead of waiting for some furniture delivery, like Dr. Emmett wanted, Celeste had been more daring, less appropriate, and loud as hell.

"Well, Max, when you stop doing all the shit you do, I'll cut out my fucking attitude, OK?"

He scoffed but said nothing.

She walked into the office this morning assuming that she'd have to face consequences for that. For fuck's sake, she'd said it within earshot of patients in the lobby. Ain't no way Dr. Emmett wouldn't reprimand her in some way for that. He was a good sport, as long as it was all in good fun, but she had crossed a line. And she knew it. That's why she didn't look back at him on her way out the door. But, for God's sake, she always got Marcus from JV basketball practice on Wednesdays. Dr. Emmett was just being a pill because he had one of those boys waiting on him in the parking lot. This latest one had no game whatsoever. That kid always parked in the same place. She didn't dare tell Dr. Emmett she knew about any of that, though. Those are the kinds of secrets you keep for a rainy day.

Dr. Emmett thought he was good at keeping down low, but, after two years of being his nurse, the only one who stuck around, there was nothing that Celeste didn't know about him. He could bitch at her all the time if he wanted, how "inappropriate" she was, that HIPAA nonsense he was always on about when she got to know the patients and asked them about their lives. She could put up with a lot of stuff, turn a blind eye to some shenanigans, so long as he kept paying her well. She could block out when he whined. Dr. Emmett was white noise. Very white noise. Just let him try and threaten her job, though, and Dr. Emmett would see how quickly storm clouds would brew.

Instead of rushing to work and facing whatever headache of busy work he had prepared as "punishment," Celeste tried her best to have a leisurely Thursday morning. She woke up and watched a makeup tutorial. Listened to the end of a mystery audiobook—and predicted the ending again. She took Marcus to breakfast at Hardee's before school. She filled up the Olds with gas.

Let Dr. Emmett unlock the office. Let him turn on all the lights. Let him figure out how to walk around a new, stupid, unnecessary white couch while scanning all those records, if he could walk after his "date" last night.

When Celeste finally showed up for work, sauntering in about ten minutes after the office was supposed to open, she was primed to raise hell if Dr. Emmett gave her any grief. Instead, the front door was unlocked, but the waiting area was dark. That new couch was just randomly placed in the middle of the room, still wrapped in the plastic. Receipt on it. It was unlike Dr. Emmett to leave that sort of thing undone. The man was so persnickety, he was practically a stereotype. If there was still plastic on it, that's how he wanted it.

She looked at the receipt for delivery, put it in her pocket. He'd want her to scan it for taxes. He'd also want her to unwrap the thing and make it look as pretty as the rest of his beloved New York waiting room. For a moment, she considered that he maybe left the plastic down so that he could christen the couch with his little date. But she didn't want to think about that shit.

Or touch it.

The lights behind the reception desk weren't on, either. Maybe Dr. Emmett was running late himself. Or hiding from her, waiting to pounce.

She called out to him. Nothing.

So, Celeste thought, screw him and his dumb jokes. She didn't have time for this kind of passive-aggressive white nonsense. She hmphed and proceeded to her desk, even though no morning in Dr. Emmett's office had ever started like this. Patients were about to show up, if anyone followed medical instructions and actually showed up 15 minutes before their actual appointment time.

Celeste saw the problem as soon as she walked through the door. He lay face down in front of the desk, a bloody gash in his bald spot, surrounded by his blond crown of hair. Some of his blood had pooled on the floor around his head. He was surrounded by paper. And she didn't scream. She didn't freak out. There was no time for hesitation. She knew what needed to be done, and she did it. Find his pulse. Mouth-to-mouth. Chest compressions. Talking to him, saying his name, trying to get him awake. She sang "Stayin' Alive" by the Bee Gees to assure she gave the right amount of thrusts. She used his Christian name, tried to sound warm.

"Max...," she spoke, hoping it wasn't futile to do so. She reached for her phone, tried to unlock it. She kept at the compressions. He was alive. Please be alive. He was alive.

The front door jingled behind her. The patient was early. Celeste turned toward her, told her firmly to call 911, all while keeping up the compressions. Then she breathed into his mouth. This was what needed to be done right now, not any questions about how this all happened. He wasn't Dr. Emmett. She wasn't his employee. There was no division between them. They needed to connect. They needed to survive. There's an intimacy to saving a life. She knew he had to be touched. He had to be kissed. She had to reach him, wherever he was, if she could. She had to believe she could succeed, even if she couldn't. Celeste worked to keep Max alive.

"Do you have those electric paddles to shock him?" the patient asked, whoever she was.

"There's a pulse," Celeste said matter-of-factly. "We don't need the paddles."

And she worked for the five minutes it took for the paramedics to arrive, the stressful, terrible, endless five minutes that feel like hours. She tried not to second-guess herself. She tried not to think her actions heroic. She just did the practical applications, the things she had been trained to do.

He wasn't a fair boss. He underestimated her. He misunderstood and dismissed her. Dr. Emmett always treated her like she had a flair for the dramatic, an unfair distinction that she let him continue to use on her. She wasn't playing at emotion. She felt it. She wasn't acting. It was real. Life could be intense, and it takes people willing to acknowledge that to do what needs to be done. If you live with extremes, they scare you less when you come face-to-face with their absolute fucking worst.

Δ

When the medics took over CPR, Celeste stepped back from the scene and began to pray for her boss. He wasn't dead. She did what she could. She prayed it was enough. She prayed for God's mercy, which she believed in and believed was deserved by everyone. Though she intentionally kept her own son from visiting her at work once Marcus hit puberty, though she suspected the kind of tastes that Dr. Emmett had, though she turned a blind eye more often than not in favor of a paycheck, Dr. Emmett did not deserve to die. He did not deserve pain. Celeste believed that.

Maybe this was the hypothetical rainy day. She couldn't keep Dr. Emmett's secrets after this. Celeste dreaded what it all meant. Dr. Emmett got bit in the ass by evil. She had to tell the cops, even if she was afraid. But she had to be careful so that evil wouldn't bite her in the ass too. Maybe. But it wouldn't look good for her or her son if word got out that she kept Dr. Emmett's secrets. She could point out that lots of people had motive, but she had motive too.

After Dr. Emmett was rushed away in an ambulance, Celeste went back to her desk and got on the phone, never mind the fire engine in the parking lot or the cops circling around. She needed to be Miss Marple—with better hair. She needed to be Poirot without the showiness.

Better to be a blank page. Celeste wanted to listen more than talk, even if she was the witness, even if she was the hero.

She pulled up the day's appointments on her computer and began dialing the phone.

Every appointment needed to be postponed before people started showing up annoyed and pissed off to an office with no dentist.

Celeste waited for the cops to come ask her questions, and one of them eventually did. Some chirpy girl who didn't look like she could find a toy in a Cracker Jack box, let alone any facts in this situation.

"How did you find him?"

"He was face down on the floor in front of my desk, surrounded by papers. He was hard to miss. I flipped him over, gave him CPR."

"He looked like he banged his head pretty hard," the cop said.

"Yes," Celeste agreed. "Hit his head on the desk, probably. I've done it before."

"Was anything out of the ordinary when you walked in?"

"My boss was face down on the ground for God knows how long. And, um, there was a new couch."

"New couch?"

"The one wrapped in plastic in the lobby. The cream-colored one. They were supposed to deliver it yesterday. I guess they did it last night or this morning."

"I'll go check it out."

"OK," Celeste said. "May I continue calling our patients to tell them about the accident?"

The chirpy cop nodded.

Celeste spoke into the phone to another answering machine.

"Mrs. Foster, this is Celeste from Dr. Emmett's office. He won't be seeing patients this week due to an emergency."

The cop wandered away. Cops are dumb.

Celeste just called down the list, first today's patients, then tomorrow's. And then the next day's. Looking over the couch, the cops left a business card, then left the scene. They'd check on him at the hospital, they said.

Agreed it looked like an accident. Said they'd reach out if they had any questions. It was all far more painless than Celeste feared it might be. Life is never like the movies.

Δ

Maybe an hour after everyone had left her alone, Celeste dug the delivery receipt out of her pocket, glanced at the signature at its base. Wade Emmett. Wade Emmett? Stupid, stupid kid.

She added a call to the end of her roster, finding the patient's phone number in the database. There were only so many Wades. And she remembered Wade Harrell, the hilarious boy who kept talking about how beautiful Dr. Emmett was. She still had that video on her phone.

The call went directly to the kid's voicemail. Celeste played it cool.

"Hi Wade, this is Celeste at Dr. Emmett's office. I see you have a cleaning scheduled on the second to never, and I just wanted to touch base with you. Dr. Emmett will be unavailable for any appointments. But I suspect you knew that. Call me back on my cell number. 404-945-1870. Unless you want trouble."

CHAPTER FOURTEEN

THE LITTLE BOY WHO USED TO HOLD HER HAND TO CROSS THE STREET, HUG HER TIGHT AND WHISPER HIS SECRETS IN HER EAR WAS GONE, AND MARY HARRELL DIDN'T KNOW HOW THAT QUITE HAPPENED, HOW HE RETREATED AND WAS REPLACED BY THIS SAD, ANGRY JACKASS HELL-BENT ON DESTROYING HIS LIFE DAY AFTER DAY. She thought she was watching him the whole time. She thought she was being a good mom, handling everything that was within her control. She loved him so much, and the world went and shattered them both anyway, like it was just a natural progression of events for a mother and son to schism.

The big things that broke Wade to pieces were clear, she couldn't control those. Mary couldn't halt time or puberty. He had been too sweet and sensitive. He was scared of the geese at the lake, but he couldn't help but stare at them, nervously tossing them crumbs. He didn't ride his bike when he got old enough or go out and play much. He stayed inside, read comics, and did his drawings. He liked shiny things and Wonder Woman. She let him like what he liked, but she feared the world would devour him. And it did.

She couldn't stop Lydon from dying. All her medical knowledge. All her homework. She couldn't spare her family from that kind of tragedy. The tumors were too aggressive, the pain stealing too much of her husband's good mood. Her Wade sitting in hospital rooms, old enough to know that his dad was really sick. No one gets old enough to not take death personally, though. Mary took it very personally that her husband, her partner, her boyfriend, the goofy- faced guy from the dining hall, was just stolen right out from under her.

She should've taken Wade and run from this town, but the therapists said not to disrupt life with too much change. But she should've run. They had the money. They could've gone someplace new, not been the family with the hole in it that everybody knew about. She should've spared Wade the townspeople's good intentions, the cruel bullies at school, the church invitations, the casseroles, the preacher's daughter treating him like her mascot.

Things maybe wouldn't have been perfect if they'd gone North or West, but the sort of trouble that Wade found himself in around a town like Waverly was just so, so cliché. Mundane problems annoyed Mary. He had such potential. He was such a kind little boy.

He stopped drawing when his dad died. He used to keep his pencils and sketch pad in his favorite kitchen hiding place. Mary would pretend not to notice or panic when her little tween would climb up the kitchen cabinets and reach with all his might for his special cabinet. When Lydon died, Wade made a big show, about a week after the funeral, of throwing out anything that made him happy, as though forcing a sad ending might bring about a conclusion to that chapter.

That Jessa had come to the funeral to watch her own father preach. Mary watched as the girl talked with

Wade during the reception, offering him a chicken leg and some pie. At the time, Mary felt grateful to the girl, thinking that it was good for her son to have a friend that he could talk to about life. Mary didn't have the capacity to be suspicious then.

Trying to prove something about himself or to himself—and Mary suspected maybe both—their lives were now a Southern fried daytime talk show. Illegitimate babies. Slutty preacher's kids. Uncontrolled impulses. Disappearing for hours. Teen pregnancy. Fist fights. School suspensions. And now bee-sting emergencies on the Baptist Church lawn.

Why? Why was this their life now? Sometimes she imagined how Lydon would have dealt with any of this, but she kept thinking that, if Lydon was alive, there wouldn't be any of this. Any of it.

Mary knew her son. This wasn't her son. He had such potential. Mary wasn't much of a poker player. She couldn't hide her disappointment from him, even though she tried to plaster on a smile, even though she loved her grandbaby, even though she knew he was in pain.

She wasn't a bad mother. She repeated that in her head whenever something new came up, whenever she had to learn some new way to cope. It felt unoriginal to worry about that.

Like, does anyone ever think they're a good mother for longer than a few moments before something comes along and blasts that notion almost immediately?

He wasn't answering her calls today. Not about the suspension. Not about the baby. Wade was impossible to discipline anymore. And Mary didn't know whether it was possible for her or even allowed for her to raise anyone who now had his own family. But he was only 17. And she wanted to believe that her sensitive boy was still in there somewhere, that he could still be reached.

Δ

When Mary was paged to the emergency room about the baby that morning, she rushed down to see what exactly had happened to Lydie. She expected to see Wade or someone from the daycare in the Triage area. Instead, she found, of all people, that son of a bitch Rev. Lancaster waiting down there, teary-eyed and pale. Walking through the automatic doors, she locked eyes on him first. And he shuddered, likely remembering their last unpleasant interaction. She didn't nod at him. She walked instead to get Lydie's chart from her friend Stephanie, who was pulling an on-call shift at the ER nurse's station.

Mary raised her eyebrow at Stephanie on her way toward, hoping for a hint about her granddaughter's condition. Stephanie shook her head and offered up the records. Mary glanced over them only a moment, determining that epinephrine had been administered, before Jessa rushed over in a loud and hysterical panic.

"I don't know, Jessa," Mary said to the girl. "I'm looking now. Give me a moment. You already saw the doctor, right? What'd the doctor say?"

Jessa didn't seem as interested in her daughter's condition as she was in not being blamed for it.

"It was an accident, Mrs. Harrell," Jessa blurted. "I swear it was an accident."

Mary sighed. Stephanie just sat down at the desk and began examining her own manicure with a tremendous, unbroken intensity. She'd heard about this girl, and now she was getting a front-row seat to "The Jessa Show." Mary never understood why Wade was such a fan. No quality of sex could be worth all of Jessa's extremely extra tendencies. Mentioning those traits, though, just annoyed the boy.

Lately, Wade did seem gone a little more often, though. When Mary and Jessa would pass the baby back and forth, one would ask the other where Wade was. Sometimes, neither one of them knew. Mary didn't question small blessings. She knew her boy loved his daughter. She knew he wasn't an absentee father. She just figured his occasionally flaky, distracted way had to do with him being a typical teenage boy.

Even if Wade was right here, Jessa would still be unloading on her. All the families worried about their loved ones did. It was one of the perks of being an LPN.

"Mrs. Harrell, please," Jessa whined. "Tell me what you can as soon as possible."

Lydie kept crying, her face flushed.

"Go sit down, for God's sake," Mary said, taking Jessa by the shoulders and physically aiming her toward a chair.

At this, Jessa herself looked stung. But she did as she was directed. Then, Mary turned back to Stephanie and asked more questions about her granddaughter's condition. And, completing that aspect of investigation, she went to find the on-call physician.

Δ

When Mary returned 30 minutes later with some Cheetos for Jessa, Lydie had been moved to an exam room for observation. The young mother was trembling, yet her father wouldn't even reach out and take her hand. Perhaps it was enough that he was in the room with her. Lydie just kept staring at the strange man. Mary couldn't quite blame her granddaughter for being confused.

"They're going to keep her overnight for observation, just in case," Mary said. "Nothing to worry about, probably, but she's so little."

Jessa just stayed quiet, staring at the baby.

"Praise Jesus," Rev. Lancaster said, the first thing he'd said to Mary at all in months. She glared at the man.

"Why are you here, Eric?"

"Jessa was visiting me at work when this happened."

"Jessa was visiting *you*? How did that happen at all? From what she's told me and Wade, you two haven't spoken in months."

Jessa interjected, "Mrs. Harrell, can you just—not—right—"

Mary turned to her.

"I'm sorry, Jessa, but no. I have to do this right now because, like, who knows if we'll see your father again? So, yes, I have to tell him right now that he's a piece of shit for abandoning his daughter and his grandchild. For all his so-called ethics, he's a small man, all about appearances. He has no decency when it comes to a crisis."

Rev. Lancaster shook his head, as though he was dazed from being hit in the face.

"I'm here," he said.

"Yeah, now. When something happened on your watch, the one time you were ever on watch. Where you been?" Mary asked. "You gonna reimburse me any of the cost I've incurred housing and feeding your damn kid, Eric?"

"You didn't have to do any of that," Rev. Lancaster blasted. "I don't owe you anything."

Jessa flushed. "Where was I supposed to go, Daddy?"

"Jessica, just don't."

"No, really, Reverend, where would you have your daughter go?"

"Away from your son a year ago."

Mary scoffed back at him, "It wasn't my son's idea."

"Then he's not like any boys I've ever known."

"Maybe he's not," Mary said. "Ask your daughter."

Jessa blanched.

"And where is Wade now, anyway?" Rev. Lancaster spouted. "Since he left his baby in a locked car alone this morning, maybe he's glad she's in the hospital now."

"What are you even talking about?" Mary asked.

"Your son left his baby unattended in a locked car this morning and then ran back in the house to watch cartoons or something," Rev. Lancaster repeated. "Jessa told me a neighbor had to bust out the window."

Mary looked to Jessa, but the girl wouldn't meet her eye.

Mary couldn't take it. She just walked out on both of them. They could do what they wanted with assigning blame and accusations. Mary had rounds to do.

Δ

Mary kept texting Wade throughout her shift in intensive care on Eight West, but there was no word. It sounded like he'd had the weirdest morning. After lunchtime, which she ate alone in a stairwell rather than go another round with the damn Lancasters, Stephanie called up to say someone new was being moved to her department for observation. Severe head trauma, immediate surgery, non-responsive. Coma from brain swelling.

Patient's name was Emmett, Maxwell. Mary recognized it immediately. This town was entirely too small.

Dr. Emmett showed up around 4 p.m., and Mary was helping the orderlies transfer him into one of her beds. She talked to the dentist like he was awake, the way she always did with unresponsive patients. It helps to treat them with respect.

"Dr. Emmett, I'm going to give you the quality of care you deserve," she said to him as he was lifted into the bed. She made sure his IV was working properly, that the bandages around his head were secure.

"You're a good guy," she said to the dentist. "We'll treat you well."

Her watch began to vibrate against her wrist. She checked it, thinking that she'd maybe just hit her steps goal for the day. But she had finally gotten a text back from Wade.

"Sorry. Fell asleep," it said. "What happened to the baby?"

She texted back, for Dr. Emmett wouldn't notice or care that she was texting in his state of consciousness. Hell, Dr. Emmett wouldn't notice if a marching band came through the room.

"Jessa is your problem, not mine," Mary wrote. "Get your ass to the hospital now. Lydie's under observation in Pediatric Intensive Care. My shift ends at 6. GET HERE ASAP. HER FATHER IS HERE. I HOPE HER MOTHER DOES NOT COME TOO. You are NOT leaving me alone with those damn hypocritical trash people. I WILL KILL SOMEONE."

CHAPTER FIFTEEN

DREAMING ABOUT DR. EMMETT WASN'T A NEW THING. For months, the man had taken up residence in Wade's subconscious teasing him, stripping him, feeding him, mocking Jessa, switching places with her in his dreams. But today's dreams ended with a shock of violence. Wade smacked the dream dentist across the face. His skull rolled off his head and shattered upon the ground, like it was made of porcelain.

Wade awoke with a start from his forced, lengthy slumber, and he felt normal for a moment, a side effect of being well-rested in a quiet house. For a few moments, the room blacked out except for some slight light creeping past the edge of the blinds, he forgot what time he'd gone to sleep or even what time it was.

That sensation did not last.

First, he considered his dream. Then, he looked over toward the crib. Wait, where was the baby? Where was his phone?

Scooping himself out of the mattress, putting the soles of his feet on the tough basement carpet, he forced himself upright. He had to piss. He had to get on with life. He had to rejoin the mess.

He hit the power button on the iPhone, left it on the desk attached to the charger and went to the toilet. Almost immediately upon waking, the phone began vibrat-

ing alerts to him. It did not stop. When Wade finished using the bathroom, the phone kept buzzing for nearly two
minutes. It was 3:58 p.m. It was Thursday, maybe. He
was afraid to touch the damn thing, wondering if World
War III had somehow begun or the zombie apocalypse or
some shit.

Instead, to his annoyance, it was all just personal
chaos.

First thing he noticed was the voicemail from the dentist's office. He hit play and listened to Celeste's voice.
And it returned him to Hell. What did she want? What
did she know? This was too much. He dialed the number back, but it just rang and rang, going to that stupid
cheery voicemail for Dr. Emmett's office. No matter how
many times he'd called the man, he never got used to the
sing-songy voice his lover used on the outgoing message
from his office.

"We don't negotiate with terrorists." He remembered
that from the news.

The whole thing pissed him off. Wade was never
going to stop running from this, he feared. He shouldn't
run. Particularly not from some damn dental assistant.

"Look," he said into the phone message. "I don't know
what you think you know, lady. But you better keep your
fucking mouth shut. I'm not scared of you. DON'T CALL
ME AGAIN."

He hung up the phone, felt bold for a moment, and
then that bravado just left him like so much hot air.
He wasn't dangerous. It was an act. Hitting the dentist

hadn't made him bloodthirsty. It frightened him. Wade felt like a goddamn chickenshit.

The voicemails from his mom and Jessa, basically repeated all of the stuff that their texts said in caps lock. The baby was in the hospital. There was a bee sting. It was probably nothing, but they were keeping Lydie overnight. Though Jessa sounded frantic, Wade reasoned to himself that she always sounded like that. His mom was a medical professional. She sounded more reasonable but mostly pissed off.

Should he take a shower? No, they'd be upset if they found out he hesitated at all. They'd want him to treat it like it was an emergency, but the past couple days had made him immune to emergencies, he hated to think it. But everything was shit. So, what was even the point of caring at all?

Wade pulled on a T-shirt and some underwear. He texted his mom. When he found his jeans, he also looked over his missed calls. The one unknown number was probably the hospital, so he dialed it back, just so he could find out what room he should go to. Or maybe it was some bill collector.

The answer came on the first ring.

"Hi Wade," a cheery voice said quickly.

"Hi, who's this?"

"I'm Trevor, the guy with the couch yesterday," the voice said. "I hope you don't mind me reaching out. I just—"

The guy with the couch. The pretty one. The one with the gaze that wouldn't leave him. The guy he lied to.

"Look, Trevor, I can't talk right now. I gotta go."

"Oh, OK—"

Trevor sounded upset.

"How did you get this number?"

"You sort of gave it to me," Trevor said. "Sort of—"

"Well, yeah, I wanted to talk to you again. Maybe coffee or something."

Wade paused.

"This isn't a good time, Trevor."

"It could be, Wade," Trevor said, a bit boldly. "If you're having a bad day, I can totally relate."

"All I have are bad days," Wade muttered.

Through the phone, Wade heard Trevor sigh.

"Preach," Trevor said.

Wade, in spite of himself, chuckled.

"Say Wade," Trevor continued. "I live right near your dad's office. Whenever you like, I could come by, pick you up and make your day a little better. I'm good at that. I promise."

The earnest confidence in Trevor's voice was kind and seductive, almost in equal measure, but all Wade could think about was Trevor showing up at the dentist's office, telling Celeste or anybody about the couch delivery.

"Don't go there," Wade said.

"Really? Because, if it meant seeing you again, I'd get a root canal." Wade smiled.

"Thanks for not saying you wanted any cavities filled," Wade joked.

Trevor replied quickly, "Dude. No."

"Oh, I'm sorry, I thought we were doing a thing."

"Oh, not what I mean," Trevor said. "I wouldn't want your dad filling any of my cavities. This isn't a porno."

Wade gasped, then chuckled. Who the hell was this Trevor?

"See," Trevor replied. "I knew we were flirting. You have got to get coffee with me now."

"Um."

"I'm just going to call you back 'til you say yes," Trevor said with the certainty of someone in one of Jessa's teen romances. "This is going to happen. You know it is. You know it'll be great. Come on."

Since Trevor wasn't to be dissuaded and since he wanted the guy nowhere near the dentist's office, Wade dared complicate his life even more.

"Fine, I work at the Super Kroger tomorrow night 'til 11."

"Late-night donuts and sensual massage at 11:05 then," Trevor asserted. "I'll see you in the parking lot."

The phone clicked.

Δ

Trevor's last sentence was a phrase that struck Wade as entirely too familiar. Given how things had worked out with the last guy, Wade should probably just let the delivery man down easy.

Wade put on his sneakers and walked out into the yard. Wade heard the pounding before he rounded the house. It was a knock, an insistent and angry knock. He crossed the front lawn, headed toward his car. But it was blocked in by an Oldsmobile. The trash bag in his window was already flapping in the wind from where someone had pulled on it. On his mother's doorstep, that assistant Celeste, braids askew from her terrible day, crazy eyes, wearing Miss Piggy scrubs to cover her ample frame, was banging on the door with her open hand.

He froze in his tracks, unsure of which direction to run, but he didn't get the chance.

Celeste turned her head toward the footsteps on the grass, and she saw him. She glared at him with an intensity he was unprepared to match. He could talk tough on the phone, but, faced with her, Wade was more than a little scared. She held all the cards. And he knew it.

"We need to talk about Dr. Emmett, kid," Celeste said to Wade. "Right. Fucking. Now."

"I don't know what you're talking about," Wade spat.

Celeste rolled her eyes and said, with a chuckle, "Bitch, please."

And she stepped off the front stoop, on to the lawn and walked up to him like they were gunfighters in a Western. He pretended like they weren't, though.

"I'm sorry," he said, speaking with the unearned confidence of an entitled white boy. "I've got to go to the hospital right now."

"The hospital?" Celeste asked. "Oh, little man, you gonna finish the job?"

She knew. All of it, she knew. He knew she knew. And whatever happened next was up to her.

CHAPTER SIXTEEN

WADE EYED CELESTE AS THOUGH SHE WERE A THREAT, AND THERE WAS A GLINT IN HIS EYE THAT LEGITIMATELY SCARED HER. She hadn't thought of him as threatening before, for he was just some boy. And she realized that maybe showing up at his house and confronting him about assaulting her boss maybe hadn't been the best idea. She intended him no harm. In fact, she felt guilty about him. Still, Celeste considered him a boy. She forgot that boys could be dangerous. Even seeing Dr. Emmett on the ground, bleeding from the head, she didn't think that the boy who probably did that to the man was a threat. Looking him in the eye, though, for the first time in months, Celeste realized that he could hurt her. If she played this wrong, if they were alone, if he felt threatened, he could attack her and crush her. Wade was not to be underestimated.

He didn't know that she meant him no harm. He only knew that she held information about him that he wanted no one at all to know.

She couldn't really even tell him that she meant no harm. Meaning harm and doing harm were two different consequences. And she had caused harm to him all these months without meaning to do any. If he did the math in his head, he could maybe figure out how she played a role in his current predicament. But, then, she figured no kid would want to do math for no reason.

Wade wouldn't hurt her on his front lawn, not with the neighbor being so much of a busybody. And there was probably no way that she would follow him into the house. He couldn't get the upper hand on her. So, instead of taking her on, the two of them were stuck there, and they had to continue talking it out.

Apparently, Wade's front lawn was ground zero for confrontations today, he thought. Lanky boy fights angry neighbor. Lanky boy fights girl in towel. Lanky boy versus lady in scrubs.

Because of every step that had led them there, neither of them wanted to do that. They'd both seen enough movies and read enough detective stories to know to avoid long, drawn-out speeches explaining the plot, so they spoke in staccato.

"Look," he said.

"What?"

"I can explain."

"I don't doubt you can."

"Why are you here?" he asked her.

"To see you."

"Why?"

"To talk. Just talk."

"About what?"

She replied with a raised eyebrow. There was no reason to recap the story for either of them, they both knew it.

"Are you armed?" she asked him.

"Why would I tell you that? Are you?"

"Good point."

They paused. Wade spoke first. "Dr. Emmett and I were—"

"I know who I work for," she said. "You weren't the first."

This legitimately surprised Wade. His mouth twitched from nerves.

"Oh, baby, did you think you were special?" she asked him.

He couldn't tell if she was sympathetic or mocking him. All those months ago, when she had driven him home from his surgery, during that whole weird exchange, Celeste had mocked him. He didn't trust her.

Celeste was in a predicament. When everything she said sounded sarcastic, when people had treated her like she was "sassy" since she was a girl because she was black and round, there was no tool in her arsenal of defenses that allowed her to be completely sincere.

"I'm serious, baby. Did you think you were his first?"

"Stop calling me that," Wade said. "Stop calling me baby."

"I mean nothing by it," Celeste said. "It's just how I talk."

Wade took a breath.

"He's not a nice man, Wade," she said to him. "Especially to boys like you."

Wade trembled, exposed.

"I have to go to the hospital," he said to her. "My baby daughter is there."

"You have a daughter?"

"Yes, ma'am," he told her.

135

"How does that work?"

"Not so well," Wade admitted to Celeste.

He indicated her Oldsmobile.

"Can you move your car?"

"I'll drive you to the hospital," she said. "After all, I should go check on my boss there. If you killed him, I'm out of a job."

"I didn't kill him."

"Oh really? You going to tell me that the guy from IKEA or whatever did it?"

"Dr. Emmett isn't dead," Wade said. "I didn't kill him."

"Not for lack of trying. Boy, I ain't stupid. You know what I meant. You got into it with him last night, and you banged him up."

"How do you know that?" Wade scoffed, even though he didn't have a leg to stand on.

Wade knew he'd been clumsy. He wanted to know which mistakes she'd caught.

"You signed the damn furniture delivery slip with your own first name, jackass," Celeste said. "It wouldn't take Miss Marple to solve this one."

"You shouldn't have come here," Wade asserted to her.

"And you shouldn't be messing around with old men. We all make mistakes."

Wade's phone began to buzz, interrupting the stand-off.

"Wade, let me drive you to the hospital, and we can figure out what we're going to do next," Celeste said.

"Are you going to turn me in?"

Celeste hesitated before speaking, which made Wade exceedingly nervous.

"The truth is complicated in this case," she said to him. "All I know now is that you're expected at that hospital, and I want to see Dr. Emmett with my own eyes."

She walked to the passenger side of her Oldsmobile, opening the door for him.

"I can drive my own car, Celeste."

"Nope," Celeste said. "Boy, do you think I'm a fucking idiot? We go together. I don't need you running off, getting yourself into more trouble. I want to keep an eye on you."

Wade walked over to the passenger side of the Olds, but he still felt like it was valuable to stand his ground with Celeste.

"But I can get away from you any time, lady. I have a smartphone and a rideshare app."

He waved the phone at her. This boy is dumb as hell, she thought. He was no threat. She almost felt idiotic for even worrying. Her own son never would've shown his cards so easily.

Celeste snatched the phone and put it in her pocket.

"What the fuck?" Wade asked her. "Give me that back."

"I will after you get in the damn car," she said.

Wade thought back to when they first met. "I remember you filming me when I was drugged as hell."

She bristled.

"I remember you laughing at me," he said to her.

He was doing the math, she thought.

"And it wasn't a week later, Dr. Emmett started shopping at the grocery store. All. The. Time."

"Just get in the damn car," Celeste said.

Wade stared at her, gape-mouthed like a fish, but he did as she said. She circled around the front of the Olds and then hopped into the driver's seat.

"You knew what he was, didn't you?" he asked her.

She couldn't look him in the eye.

"You're going to pay for that," he vowed. "And my phone."

She wasn't sure if he was more bothered about the phone or if he was sore that she intentionally let a child predator know Wade was interested. Either way, she didn't have time for it.

"If you're just going to whine like this," she said to him, "maybe we could just go to the police."

"You think I'm just whining?" Wade shouted. "I was 16 years old!"

She wouldn't look at him, but she spat back at him, "You think they'll try you as an adult now?"

He smirked at her. She thought she was in control. But Wade knew that control is fleeting. It shifts and changes.

She revved the Olds, its sputtering engine bleating out a stench of smoke, and she backed out of the driveway. Though he had plenty to worry about and he should've been in a panic, though he didn't know what to expect, at that moment Wade felt safe with Celeste in the driver's seat. The pair of them held each other's secrets, which made them momentary, uncomfortable allies.

CHAPTER SEVENTEEN

WAITING IN WAVERLY GENERAL HOSPITAL, REV. ERIC LANCASTER COULD ONLY APOLOGIZE SO MUCH FOR HOW HE'D BEHAVED. He could only feel so guilty. He could only be a monster for so long before the whole situation became tiresome. He understood the concept of weaponized shame. It wasn't a practice he condoned, even if people occasionally thought he practiced it as a minister. Some incorrect, judgmental liberal thinkers even thought his religion ran on it. But Eric felt they were incorrect about his faith.

And he thought his daughter and Mary Harrell were basking in his punishment a bit too much, misrepresenting what had actually happened over the course of the past year. But he'd learned from raising teenage girls in this day and age that a man corrects or instructs a woman at his own peril. So, he didn't tell Jessa she was in any way wrong about the way things had happened. Eric just remembered the events differently, and he kept these thoughts to himself while she glared at him, shouted at him or kept a tally in her head of how many times he touched or looked at the baby.

Eric knew his daughter. She was not a subtle creature. You were either with her or you were her enemy.

It was true that Eric hadn't met Lydie before today. But it wasn't like he had never set eyes on her before. Actually, he and his wife Rachel kept regular tabs on the baby through Jessa's frequent Instagram photos. They hadn't "liked" any of the images. They didn't dare give their daughter the satisfaction, but he did have a number of screencaps saved on his phone.

Instagram didn't do her enough justice. Lydie was a truly beautiful baby, the spitting image of her mommy, except Lydie had Wade's unfortunate nose. Of all the gene pools that his lovely daughter could've taken a dip in, why on Earth she would choose to be with that Harrell kid? Eric knew the answer, but he was still baffled by her choices. Jessa liked Wade because he had no spine. She did not react well to being challenged. Knowing that, he still couldn't respect the little jackass. Wade had been a whiny little boy, and now he was a sad, worthless teen.

Granted, the boy had no father, and that was sad. But Eric just didn't like him. Wade was a weirdo, and he seemed a little gay.

Eric hadn't "abandoned" his daughter. That part, Jessa and Mary kept getting wrong. He knew where she was from the moment she'd left home, shacked up in some basement with that Wade. It wasn't that she got pregnant, though the Lancasters weren't in any way happy about that as it unfolded.

She says they kicked her out, maybe even believed it with her way of revising the past so that she was always victimized, but it was untrue. The way Jessa stormed her way out of their house, Eric couldn't very well just let her back in the door without her doing some serious coming-to-Jesus. Jessa had yet to apologize to her mother Rachel. Instead, she showed up at the church today, kicking in a door and raising the same sort of hell.

Δ

The incident in the living room from eight months ago had been seared into Eric's brain.

"You two are a bunch of hypocrites," Jessa had yelled approximately three minutes after telling them that she was pregnant. "I know that the two of you didn't wait 'til you got married! And now this happened to me, and you act like there's no room at the fucking inn!"

"We said nothing to you about it," Eric had said. "Your poor mother hasn't even stopped crying yet, and you DARE compare yourself to the Mother of God? Are you kidding me with this right now?"

"You two are a bunch of racist, closed-minded liars!" Jessa yelled. "Christians, my ass! You support putting babies in cages, so why should I expect any different from you when it comes to my pregnancy?"

Tears continued to stream from Rachel's face, her sobs made her breathing erratic. Jessa stormed up the steps and began angrily packing a bag. Eric just watched as his daughter continued to set fire to every bit of good will he was willing to show her.

"You are such a liar, Daddy," she spat. "You are nicer to strangers than you are to me. All you want from me is to be your little fucking pageant princess. Well, Daddy, I'm no princess!"

"Have you been drinking? The hell is this?" he asked her, voice raised. "You're acting like we're in 'Footloose,' Jessa."

Jessa smirked at him, but joking only threw fuel on the fire, rather than douse her indignation.

"Fuck you, Daddy."

Eric knew better than to stop his daughter's tirades. Jessa's sister had run for the hills as soon as the whole scene started, but Eric and Rachel were trapped by the circumstances of Jessa's uterus. And Jessa was making everyone pay.

"You're a whore too, Mama," Jessa yelled as she walked down the steps. "Don't you fucking look at me."

This was the language that his daughter used when things did not go her way. She used it when they wouldn't buy her the Justin Bieber album. She used it when they grounded her for bad grades. She used it when her sister upset her.

That night, Jessa stormed out, took her car and, so far as he knew, hadn't been in touch with her parents since. Dumbstruck at the time, Eric muttered that maybe Jessa had been a little upset about her own choices. And Rachel, unsure of why he would dare make a joke when they'd just lost their daughter forever, had never looked at him the same way since.

But you cannot negotiate with terrorists, especially teenage girls.

To hear her now, Jessa had been the Little Match Girl, left homeless by cruel and unforgiving parents. Jessa had fed this bogus version of events to Mary so often that Mary was defending a girl she couldn't stand. She was begging to come back, but she wasn't apologizing. She kept holding the baby in front of him, trying to get Eric to play or cuddle or something. And it was brazenly disgusting.

When the doctor needed to talk to Jessa about Lydie, Eric excused himself into the hallway. Then, he went outside to smoke and make some phone calls. (He didn't dare call Rachel and tell her any of this had happened. That was definitely an in-person conversation.) The time was almost 5 p.m.

He tried his secretary Virginia on her cell phone. She answered on the first ring.

"Hey, sorry I stormed out so quickly and never came back," he told her. "You won't believe the day I've had."

"Where are you now?" Virginia asked. "Are you still with Jessa?"

"The baby got stung by a bee, so we ended up in the emergency room."

"Oh, my goodness," Virginia exclaimed. "Is the baby OK?"

"I think so," Eric said. "The doctor is talking to Jessa now."

"I'll put a note on the bulletin that she's in the hospital," Virginia said. "I have to update it anyway."

"Who's here? Anybody I can visit? Jessa's being ... a lot right now."

Virginia consulted her computer. "Max Emmett had some kind of accident at work. Betsy Jones was supposed to have an appointment today, and she walked in on his assistant doing CPR on him. Betsy called 911 and everything."

"The dentist who only shows up on Christmas and Easter?"

"Yes."

"The guy that brings business cards?"

"That's the one."

"What kind of accident?" Eric asked.

"Well, you're at the hospital," Virginia said sarcastically. "You can find that out easier than I can. Betsy said someone probably clobbered him over a root canal."

Eric chuckled, and his secretary joined him in it. Then, ever the assistant, she told him to put his game face on before going to see the dentist.

Δ

Eric went back inside the hospital, showed his clergy card even though they knew him at the front desk, and they told him where to find his holiday-only congregant. Why not visit the heathen? The minister reasoned to himself that it was a solid good deed, something that would cleanse the soul. It got him away from Jessa. And, heck, everybody deserves grace.

Eighth floor. He took the elevator up and walked toward the dentist's room. To his surprise, just outside the dentist's hospital room, Rev. Lancaster saw Wade, who'd been missing all day long, bickering with some black lady in scrubs. The lady kept pointing at Max Emmett, and she was crying for some reason.

With his usual puzzled, gape-mouthed expression, the boy looked over the lady's shoulder and met the minister's surprised eyes. At first, Rev. Lancaster remained stone-faced as he walked up to the two, too many questions battling it out in his head, and it was fun to watch the boy squirm.

Then, a scream rose out of the hospital room, a shrill, piercing exclamation in reaction to intense pain. The dentist was convulsing and screaming, awake and in agony. Wade's attention turned toward Dr. Emmett. The woman in the scrubs looked on in terror.

CHAPTER EIGHTEEN

TRAUMA ECHOES. The impression it makes lasts long after the first impact. Folks aren't rattled just once by a particularly bad incident. They're shaken for good, like a sealed can of Coke that someone sloshes around and then returns to the shelf. There's a chance that the pressure and chemistry building up inside might dull over time, but there's no guarantee of that. There's no telling how long someone might remain volatile once they've been subjected to pain and shock. Some people endure for ages just fine. Others explode.

The three familiar faces in the doorway were frozen in shock, none of them looking away from the screams. The dentist thrashed, howling in agony only "No! No!! No!!" over and over. And Mary and an orderly built like a linebacker rushed past the gathered gawkers. Gnashing and pulling at his IV and bandages, Dr. Emmett kept grinding his head into his pillow. Quickly, Mary and the linebacker held the dentist down and put a sedative into his IV.

Max babbled, looked from Wade to Celeste to Mary. Rev. Lancaster muttered words of prayer while watching him struggle. Max should've recognized them all, but his eyes were wild, open with terror, the sockets bleeding.

"Wade, what are you doing here?" Mary shouted at him. "Get out!"

She forced everyone out of the doorway and into the Eight West hallway. Other patients passed by them, shocked looks on their faces.

The dentist stopped screaming and struggling after a moment, his bleeding eyes fixed on Wade until the door shut.

Wade gasped, feeling condemned. His mom put her arms around him to keep him from falling. And she continued to hold him back.

"Mom, why were his eyes like that?" Wade whispered half to himself. "He's all bruised up."

"You shouldn't be here, damn it," Mary glared at the three of them. "None of you should be."

"Why was he bleeding from the eyes?" Wade asked her.

"It's none of your concern, Wade," Mary said. "You know I can't tell you anything."

Rev. Lancaster stepped back a bit. Celeste was still shocked.

"Why did you all come up here?" Mary asked.

"I'm his minister," Eric said.

Celeste's head snapped angrily in his direction. "The hell you mean? Max's minister?"

"He's a member of my congregation," Eric said to her. "Who even are you?"

His tone communicated everything Celeste needed to know about him.

"Someone who doesn't have to answer you," Celeste snapped, her eyes rolling. "Max's minister. Yeah, right."

She turned toward Wade and said, "You need to talk to your mother. I'll be around."

Wade nodded at her, which puzzled everyone. Celeste, still trembling from the screams, walked down the hallway, turned and went toward God knows where. Wade knew she wouldn't go far from him. He imagined her crying in a bathroom. Celeste didn't seem the type to totally lose her cool where anyone might see.

Δ

"Explain yourself," Mary said to her son once she finally got him alone in the Eight West nurses lounge. She told Eric flatly to either go back down to Jessa and the baby or go home because Dr. Emmett wasn't in any condition for visitors. She told her co-workers she needed a break, that it would take as long as it takes.

"I don't know where to start," Wade said to his mother.

He sat in a love seat, and she pulled up a chair next to him, holding his hand while looking in his eye. It was the stance she took on the rare occasion when she had to give a patient some somber news. He didn't know if she positioned them like this on purpose. He didn't know what his mother knew about him, and he was too scared to tell her the truth, even if Celeste had urged him to spill everything.

"You can start anywhere, Wade," Mary said kindly. "Start with why you got into a fight at school."

"Huh?"

"You got suspended from school," she said.

"Oh," he said, "Right. That." So much had happened.

"What on Earth is even going on with you these days?"

"Mom, I have no idea," he said.

"That isn't going to cut it, Wade," Mary said. "I feel like I don't even know you anymore. Like, where did you even go?"

"Go?" Wade said to her. "I'm right here."

She took both of his hands in hers. "No, you're not."

"I don't understand."

No one ever said in the parenting books the heavy lifting involved with getting your child to see the point, Mary thought. There were no instructions on the right way to love him or hope for him. Too many people she knew always pretended that everything was fine with their kids, listing off things like Honor Roll and PSAT scores. Her son had a baby and, yeah, decent PSAT scores. But she felt like she hadn't spoken to him, really, in years.

Mary sighed. "You know you can tell me anything, right?"

Wade shrugged.

"You used to talk to me when something was bothering you. Now I know stuff bothers you, I can see it all over your face. So, I'm begging you right now to tell me about it."

Wade answered in a whisper, "I can't."

She answered aloud. "Yes, you really can."

Wade's brow furrowed with tension. It looked to Mary like panic. The expression was momentary, but Mary was reminded of Lydon on the day he got the cancer diagnosis.

"Wade, did you leave Lydie in the car today?"

"Who told you about that?"

"Jessa's dad, for some reason."

"Big surprise," Wade scoffed.

"Why did that happen, honey? What was going on?"

"Mom, it was nothing. Mrs. Winston totally overreacted, and she busted my damn window."

"Just tell me what happened, Wade," Mary spoke very gently. "Leave blame out of it. It makes stories so much shorter."

"My stories bore you?" Wade asked her defensively.

"That's true of everyone, honey," she said. "Doctors. Patients. Nurses. From bosses to toddlers. Everybody wants to escape responsibility for bad stuff, so they frame all their stories around why it isn't their fault. What I'm saying is that I don't care if it's your fault. I just want to know what the hell happened. I'm not mad. I'm not criticizing you. Just cut that shit out of it."

"Mom...," Wade started, whimpering a little. He shook his head. "I can't—there's too much."

"Just start with the fight," Mary said to him.

"But it doesn't start with the fight."

"That's what's important to me right now," Mary said. "That's the little thing that we can talk about. That's what we can deal with before we go check on the baby."

"That kid has been teasing me for years, Mom," Wade said. "He used to pick on me every day, calling me faggot. He stole my bookbag. I just, after the neighbor lady made me so mad, I just had to take it out on somebody."

She looked at him. There he was. She saw him. She saw the boy she recognized.

"You've had a bad time of it lately," Mary said, trying to understand.

"Lately??? Mom, he's been giving me shit for years. He said I would watch him. He said I had a crush on him. He called me weird. Said I was gay. Like, all the time. Even after Jessa..."

"Wade, do you love Jessa?" Mary asked.

"What? Why does that matter?"

"You're never home, Wade. You barely see the baby. I mean, I get it. I can't stand her either."

He laughed.

"But that's not what I'm talking about, Wade," Mary explained.

"What are you talking about?"

"Your life lately is just checked out, wandering around like you have some cloud over you. You're scared and unhappy. And now you're fighting everyone all the time."

"I don't fight everyone all the time," Wade muttered.

"You don't need to fight me, kid," Mary said. "The only time I see you happy is when you're walking from the driveway to the basement after work. The only time I catch you smiling is when I go see you at the grocery store. Once you get to the basement door, your smile disappears. It doesn't disappear with the baby. It only vanishes with that damn girl."

"What are you talking about? You watch me?"

"Of course, I watch you," Mary said. "You're my damn kid."

Wade confessed, "I thought you were mad at me. You couldn't even look at me."

"Your brain isn't fair to you, Wade," Mary told him. "You think the world is out to get you and that you can't do anything right. Your brain doesn't tell you the truth."

Wade frowned.

"Why are we talking about this now?"

"I know you don't love her, son," Mary said. "Did that boy hit a nerve with you today? Is that why you punched him?"

"Mom, are you asking me if I'm gay?" Wade asked.

"Are you?"

Wade shook his head. "I don't really—I mean—"

She caught the look on his face, deciphered it, and hugged her son. She held him tightly, as though she were keeping him safe. She wanted him to know that she was doing just that.

"It's OK," Mary said to him. "Everything's OK."

Wade hugged her back. Relief hit him for a moment. He felt like himself. And he let himself breathe. A small secret was out. His mother was on his side, and that was something good to know. Even though he knew everything was not actually OK. The bloody eyes of Dr. Emmett, angry and unhinged, filled with blame, would never leave him be.

CHAPTER NINETEEN

MAX THOUGHT HE WAS ACCUSTOMED TO PAIN, SINCE HE PRACTICALLY TRADED IN IT AS A DENTIST. He thought he knew suffering. But the terror and the hammering, shuddering, startling mix that hit him now drove him mad with its cruelty. Since yesterday—*was it yesterday? How long had it been*—Max was more than just sore. He more than ached from the head. It wasn't a stabbing. It wasn't a sting. It was a heat, a burning, echoing from his brain, like his hand—no, his head—was on a stove, and he couldn't lift it off.

Max was nowhere. No time passed. Everything hurt.

Whatever Wade had clobbered him with, it knocked him free from everything he knew. He visualized himself reliving memories. He imagined himself strapped to his own dentist chair, surrounded by a blur of others, judging him for his crimes. The judges—voices he knew, faces he didn't—wanted to condemn him.

It was never a dream. It was always real. Max could pinch himself in it and feel it, and he couldn't reason his way out of it, the way you can puzzle your way free from sleep by asking yourself questions about the situation. Max asked all the questions, shown moments from his childhood, from his bad boyfriends, from the past two months. He wouldn't wake up. He wondered if he was in death. He wondered if he was in hell. Hell had a dentist's chair.

Hell was a flash of memories, all of them bad. And the judges showed them to him, the chair venturing like a roller coaster from nightmare to nightmare, Max could not move from them and could not blink.

Sometimes he could make himself budge, and he'd feel himself, eyes suddenly open, in a pool of blood on the floor of his office. Then, in a flash, it would be gone. He would try and grab for anything, knocking over papers, but then he'd be gone from the office floor, back in the dentist's chair, watching porn with his Uncle Charlie when he was 10, the man's hand upon his knee.

Max would flash to the sounds of a bone saw, a nurse telling him not to worry, and then he'd hear his own drill, the whizzing and the high-pitched squeal it made as a little boy winced and squirmed under the weight of it. Even through laughing gas, the little boys—baby squishy ones of about 5 or 6—would still wince and squirm, trying to stop more than pain. The boys would try to stop the idea of pain, the promise of pain. They didn't want to learn what pain had to teach them. The painkillers made them sillyheads, too. They were all cute and pliable and funny-sounding.

"Is this real life?" the little patient would ask him, the drugs turning him from a man into a Muppet.

Max asked himself this now. Max asked his judges this.

"Is this real life?" Max screamed, and the judges towered over him. They told him no.

Max never touched the littlest ones. He would only entertain the ones who wanted to be entertained, the ones like Wade who were old enough to understand how good it felt to be touched before Max touched them. Like Christopher. Like Jacob. He'd been that age when he was taught it. And it hadn't messed him up. He was preparing them for life. They'd walk away, at 16 or whatever, laid and experienced.

The state allowed it. If Wade had been a girl, he could consent. Georgia was a bit murkier about the gays, though. At one point, it didn't want the guys fucking each other, no matter the age at all.

Max cared about Wade. He flashed, while in the dentist chair, to Wade crying about his dad, to Wade crying about his baby, to bitching about something. Wade was just a crybaby, perpetually in need, always crying. Sometimes it was nice to save such boys. Sometimes it was just a headache.

Other boys weren't like Wade, the 18-year-olds he met on the Internet, the 20-year-old college kids. They were stronger. Those dalliances never lasted as long. Max was never their first time, just the first time they'd tried someone older. Max knew how to kiss them, knew how to touch them. Max liked to be a teacher, though. He liked his partners to learn things.

The conversations with the judges, the moments, would last for hours. They'd be boring or painful, inescapable. Max would struggle against the straps on the dentist's chair, and the whirring of the drill would threaten him.

"We suffer through," a judge whispered, sounding like Celeste. "You suffer. You suffer for what you've done."

"What about you, Celeste?" Max screamed into the void. "What about what you did? You brought that boy to me."

"He is just a boy," the judge whispered.

"You know you know."

The scenes continued to play, the moments where he asked Uncle Charlie to touch him, after he knew how it would feel. Max used to want to tell his secrets, but what could Uncle Charlie say in reply? Uncle Charlie could say Max did it and wanted to do it.

Max took responsibility for the things that happened to him. He encouraged Wade to do the same. When he kissed Wade, Wade kissed him back. There was a willingness. But there was more. Max liked control.

When Max saw the night in the hotel, he felt himself biting Wade's ear, dragging his tongue along the boy's chest. Wade had said it was better than sex with that girlfriend of his. Wade said everything was good. And Max tried to feel like he'd done something decent, romantic and spontaneous by taking the boy away with him.

Δ

In a flash, a jolt of pain brought Max's eyes open, and he saw blood in front of his eyes.

And Wade. And Celeste. And they were standing there, staring at him, terrified of what they saw. Max screamed. And they seemed to hear him. They saw the blood just as he did.

They told him he was awake. They marveled at each other that Max was awake. He wasn't in a dentist chair. He was in a hospital bed, and he jolted to try and break free from them. But it was still difficult to move.

This was hell, and they were his judges. And they had condemned him to suffer.

Wade's mother rushed in, pricking Max with needles, yelling obscenities all around the room. And Max was numb, his head on a pillow, but he still felt like screaming. He was still in hell. He was not free.

In hell, everyone knew Max's secrets, and no one shared the blame with him.

"Am I dead?" he asked Wade's mother in a whisper.

"You were in an accident," she replied. "You're in the hospital."

But the judges haunted him, standing over him. Wade's mother was just another judge.

He saw them. He looked to Wade, terrified. Celeste convulsed. And then it all faded away, leaving only the pain and the thoughts.

Max pictured the six-year-old blonde boy who squirmed in his chair, putting a hand up to try and keep the drill away, but the drugs had already taken effect. It was too late, even with the boy's hands up, to stop the pain. Max wielded pain as a way of improving lives. Pain creates better smiles.

Guilty as hell, Max thought, condemning himself. Unsure of what was real anymore, he knew only pain, he expected only pain.

Death could just be a continuation of pain, not a rest or a reprieve from it. It was a slideshow of nightmares that occasionally forced you to walk back through it, suffering in a new way. Still, Max wondered what he deserved.

CHAPTER TWENTY

COMFORT ONLY WORKS IF YOU ALLOW YOURSELF TO ACCEPT IT. Wade could tolerate only a few minutes of his mother's embrace before he had to break away. Sure, it was nice to share more about himself with her. It was nice to know that she wouldn't completely reject him if he kissed a guy. It was good to feel less alone. But after a few minutes with Mary, he just felt guilty as fuck because he was still lying to her. It's easy for her to talk about a mother's unconditional love. She didn't know her son was a monster. All her words and kindness would evaporate.

Wade said he had to go check on Lydie, whom he hadn't even seen since he came to the hospital. He said he needed to know that his baby was all right. Mary nodded, told him to go down to the ICU and see her favorite on-call nurse in the hospital, Stephanie, who would lead him to the right room. Stephanie was always where she was needed at Waverly General.

"The baby would love to see you," Mary told him. "You and I can talk more later."

She patted him on the shoulder, her way of letting him know that they were going to make their way through this. And she smiled at him. Or maybe she just smiled at the prospect of getting Jessa out of her basement. Maybe it was a bit of both, the thought of which made Wade wince.

Wade passed by Dr. Emmett's room and glanced at the man, now dozing in some painkiller haze. The dentist's head was bandaged, the circles under his eyes were severe. He looked puffy and weak. The gash in Dr. Emmett's head was still bleeding on the bandages. And Wade had done that to him.

Though he was tempted to step inside and apologize to his lover, Wade decided to look away and just keep moving toward the elevators. He couldn't risk his mother finding him there again. Besides, no apology could be enough. And even if the dentist could ever dare to forgive him, Wade would never be able to forgive himself for giving in to the impulse. He knew now what sort of person he was. He knew what it was like to bash in someone's skull. Wade knew he was the sort of person who'd just leave a man lying in his own blood.

Wade stepped aboard the elevator, hit the button for the third floor, and headed to pediatrics.

Wade was the sort of person who'd kill. He was the sort of person who'd hurt someone else. It's a terrifying thing to learn. And Wade didn't just harm any man, he harmed his lover. He tried to kill someone who had provided him with care, who had listened to him when he was stressed and down for months. In the minutes and days before yesterday, Wade considered Dr. Emmett to be the best thing in his life, a secret reprieve from everything confusing and sad.

Wade wished he were older, so that all of these emotions and the sex stuff would make more sense. If Lydie had come when he was ready for children, if he'd kissed Dr. Emmett when he was in college or whatever, all of this would be easier to deal with, Wade guessed. He envied adults. Adults knew what they were doing. His dad was always in control. His mom faced down crises at work every single day. Dr. Emmett was a successful person.

Wade saw himself as a mess of a human being, a pinball that hit every bumper, causing noise and disaster until it inevitably crashed.

He tried searching in his phone whether he could be tried as an adult or if he was still eligible for juvie, stupidly cursing himself for a second that he should've tried murder before he turned 17. But the phone wouldn't connect to the internet while he was on the elevator.

Wade put the phone back in his pocket as the door to the elevator opened. If the cops got a hold of his phone, they could check that kind of thing. That—and all the daddy porn links he'd been perusing lately—would convict him, particularly in Georgia. Georgia would just send him to the electric chair, probably.

Exiting the elevator to try to find the baby, finally, Wade instead got quite a shock.

Δ

Waiting to go up, he saw that delivery guy Trevor, holding a bouquet of flowers.

Trevor saw him and grinned.

"Hey, I was just—," the delivery man started.

Wade, with eyes opened wide, recoiled from the young man in horror. And Trevor's face dropped from the reaction.

"What are you doing here?" Wade asked. "Jeez, is everybody here today?"

"Well, I didn't mean to scare you," Trevor said. "I just heard your dad was in the hospital."

"My dad?" Wade asked, then reconsidered. "Oh yeah, he's here. How did you hear about that? Was it on the news or something?"

Idiot, Wade cursed himself. Why would a dentist falling down be on the news?

"I was making a delivery near the office, and it was shut down," Trevor explained. "Somebody at the drugstore said the dentist was in the hospital. I figured you'd be here and maybe you'd need a shoulder or something."

Wade looked at him skeptically.

"But I don't even know you," he said to Trevor, trying not to look into his eyes. Trevor's eyes were very distracting.

"I've found that barely matters when you're in a crisis," Trevor said. "A friendly face always helps."

Wade smirked at this. It had to be some kind of joke. No one was this nice. "And the flowers are for my dad?" Wade asked.

"Well," Trevor replied, blushing. "No."

"Well, I'm not sure my dad would understand a guy bringing me flowers," Wade said, then considered the irony.

"But isn't he in a coma or something?"

"Jesus," Wade said. "Do those people at CVS know everything?" Trevor laughed, and Wade snapped out of the haze.

Wade had places to go and people to see. Trevor—so shiny and nice—had this weird way of making him goofy, even in dire situations. It made no sense. Wade understood what it was and what it was about, of course, but it did him no damn bit of good to know Trevor right now. And Trevor didn't know what he didn't know. And Trevor knew enough to mess up Wade's life if he started asking the right questions.

Instead, Trevor just smiled at him.

"Look, I have to be somewhere right now," Wade said, stepping away from Trevor and the elevator.

"But isn't your dad upstairs? The front desk told me he was up there."

"Well, yeah, he is, but, like, I have to check on something else." Some thing. Wade just called his daughter a thing.

"I can come with you," Trevor said, trying to follow.

"No, dude, you really shouldn't," Wade said, grabbing the flowers and dashing away. Then he turned and asked the delivery guy, "I'm seeing you tomorrow, right?"

When Wade went toward pediatrics, Trevor stopped jogging behind him, looking a little puzzled by the whole exchange. Wade turned and headed to Stephanie. The nurses there were all in a huddle.

Stephanie turned and glared at him, looking teary-eyed and pissed. "Hi Stephanie, which room is the baby in?"

"I don't know how on Earth you can tolerate that insane young woman," Stephanie blurted at him. "She's awful."

"What do—?"

"Wade, your little girlfriend is a horrible mother," Stephanie complained.

"What happened?" Wade asked. "Where is the baby?"

"That Jessa bitch just ran off with her," Stephanie said.

"Huh?" he asked, feeling very small.

"She was trying to hurt the baby," Stephanie explained. "Seriously. I tried to stop her. And then she just screamed at me, took the baby and bolted."

Baffled, Wade turned, trying to figure out where Jessa could've taken his baby girl.

CHAPTER TWENTY-ONE

JESSA'S PHONE KEPT GOING TO VOICEMAIL. Wade had no choice but to leave the hospital to try and track her down. As he walked toward the parking lot, like he had with his mother a hundred times before, Wade remembered that his car wasn't there. He'd ridden with Celeste in her Oldsmobile. Looking around the lot, he didn't see the Olds in the place they'd parked. He didn't know where Celeste or her car had disappeared to.

Wade walked back toward the emergency room doors and opened the Lyft app on his phone. As it tracked down drivers in the area, he prayed that the driver would be some stranger. The last thing he wanted was another familiar face—some classmate or that dude Trevor, who was apparently everywhere—pulling up to help him home.

Luckily, the driver who arrived in a dark sedan had an unfamiliar face and no interest in chit-chat. The man barely spoke to Wade once the boy hopped into the backseat and shut the door.

As they exited the lot, Wade finally caught sight of Celeste. She was unloading bags of carryout from Waffle House from her car, for some reason. She was so focused that she didn't notice him pass.

It made sense to get her to like him. She could still cause him a lot of trouble, right? But she hadn't done that so far. Celeste seemed like a magic trick. She worked on people, building up their trust and compassion by actually listening to them, he figured. It was a pretty good trick, like some sort of motherhood voodoo spell she cast. It was the same sort of trick she'd used on him that day of his surgery, her warm laughter making him confess his thoughts about Dr. Emmett while she drove him home. Each time, he'd spilled most everything to her, granted most of which she already knew, and in return she'd given him nothing about herself.

He reconsidered their interaction. They argued on his front lawn about attempted murder. Then, they went to the hospital. There, she watched her boss bleed out of his eyes. Then she encouraged her boss's teenage attacker to come out to his own mom, then she just—like, huh?—apparently decided to go to Waffle House for some hash browns.

Celeste followed a path that Wade couldn't even see. He liked her for that. He'd have to ask her about it later. And he didn't doubt for one second that he would, in fact, see Celeste again later. Though it was tempting for him to think that the two of them shared a common enemy, Wade figured instead that maybe they just shared a common grief.

He looked at the clock. It was 5:37 p.m. He maybe should've waited before taking off, talked to his mother a little bit more.

But Lydie was his priority. And if Stephanie was telling the truth, that Jessa was trying to hurt Lydie, he had to save his girl. Even though he was new, even though he'd been distracted, even though he felt like a kid himself, Wade knew enough about being a parent to know that.

Wade had let himself get too distracted from Lydie. Looking at her made him feel guilty, so he stopped coming home to her. The women in his life considered him a screw-up, so he just stopped trying, fulfilling their prophecy. He should've done things differently. He should've stepped up. Lydie deserved a better father than that. He had to be more than just some 17-year-old doormat.

Δ

When Wade arrived home, Rev. Lancaster's SUV was in the Harrells' driveway, taking up so much space that there was no way around it. The reverend himself was leaning against his car, taking up more space, talking to the bitch neighbor lady so politely. Mrs. Winston must go to his church, Wade thought. It was another reason not to like her.

Wade jumped out of his Lyft and broke for his mom's part of the house, knowing Jessa probably locked their entrance to the basement. The sedan driver just pulled away like it was nothing, and Wade felt his cell phone vibrate with the notice of the end of the ride.

The reverend reached to grab him. But Wade evaded capture and bolted toward the porch.

"Hey, Wade! My daughter doesn't want to see you!"

"It's my house," Wade shouted.

He fumbled for his keys, got inside, locked the front door and moved toward the kitchen.

In spite of himself, he glanced over his shoulder at his hiding place. Wade could feel the teeth smirking at him from behind the cabinet door.

He could not stop. He had to prioritize Lydie. So, he opened the door and rushed down the basement steps, where he saw Jessa packing a fucking suitcase on the bed's bare mattress. She'd already stripped off his sweaty, stained sheets, and they sat in a pile on the floor. She glanced up at him in shock.

"You've got to be kidding me right now," he said, voice trembling.

"Don't, Wade," she said to him. "Don't. Even. Start."

"You've got to be fucking kidding me with this shit, Jessa," Wade shouted. "Like, honestly, you spent one goddamn day with the asshole, and now you want to go home with him like everything's fucking fine?"

"Do not talk. You don't get to talk."

"I can talk as much as I fucking want. You've lived here for two months while that asshole just ignored you."

"—where you became the asshole who ignored me."

Wade's face drained of color. The baby started to cry.

"We have a damn baby," she said to him. "We have a baby, and where the hell have you been all day? Jeez, where the hell are you most of the time?"

"Working," Wade said. "I have a job. And I have school. And I'm working all the fucking time."

"You don't even want me ever," she said. "We never even watch old movies anymore. We don't even have Friday night anymore."

Wade took a few steps down toward her, but Jessa stepped away from the suitcase toward the baby, not even letting him diminish the distance between them by an inch.

"I'm taking the baby, and I'm going back to my parents' house."

"Where they'll treat my Lydie like she's some sinful mistake."

Jessa's forehead wrinkled, for Wade seemed to act like Lydie was a mistake all the time. She picked up their daughter and cradled her.

"It won't be like that," she said. "If you'd seen my father today, you'd know that he's changed."

"I did see him today," Wade said, confused. "I saw him at the hospital."

"When were you at the hospital? I never saw you, Wade. For hours."

"I showed up just as you bolted, apparently," Wade admitted. "Stephanie said you were trying to hurt the baby."

Jessa just kept talking, "And then I come here, and I find the sheets all covered in lube. What the hell did you do? Jack off and sleep all day while our baby was suffering?"

"Apparently, our baby was suffering because of all sorts of shit that you did," Wade said. "Don't act all high and mighty, bitch."

"All I did was try and fix the baby's hair, and that nurse went insane," Jessa said. "Don't you ever call me a bitch again, OK? Never, ever. Fucking pervert."

"Oh really? I'm a pervert?" Wade asked. "You're the one who straddled me. I was just trying to watch an old movie. You were the one all fired up to lose your virginity."

"I care about you, Wade, you stupid idiot," she admitted. "I wanted you to touch me. I thought you wanted to touch me. We'd been spending time together for months."

Their words dueled and danced around each other. The baby's screams drowned both of them out. And Wade realized he wanted to stop.

At that moment, Rev. Lancaster began jostling the backyard doorknob, trying to break into their conversation. Wade was right. Jessa had locked everyone out. He began shouting for her to let him in.

But she just kept cradling her baby, shaking over what happened at the hospital. Wade, even though he didn't want to give her a moment's consideration or kindness, just listened. Her father, shut out, just kept pounding on the door.

Jessa took a breath.

"I was just trying to fix her hair," Jessa said to the baby and to herself. "I don't know why. She just looked all uncomfortable and in pain. I didn't want her to be uncomfortable. Singing didn't work. She was so unhappy. I can't believe the day she's had."

"But she doesn't have hair, Jessa," he said to her, softening a little.

"Oh, I know that, idiot," she replied. "I wasn't even really thinking. I just wanted to make something nicer for her."

"And so, you scraped her head with a hairbrush? Really fucking nice."

"I. Never. Touched. Her. With. The. Fucking. Hairbrush," Jessa said in a staccato fury. "I never touched her. I would never. That fucking nurse friend of your mother's just assumed the goddamn worst about me. Because she's a friend of your mother's."

"Stephanie is a completely reasonable person," Wade said. "I've known her for years."

"I don't give a fuck, Wade," Jessa said. "She's just some bitch who said I was hurting my daughter."

"Well then, why did they think you were going to hurt her?" Wade asked.

"I was going through my purse, Sherlock. I grabbed a brush. I looked at it. I was holding the baby. And the bitch nurse walked in, like I fucking said, and she yelled at me about brushing the baby's hair and threatened to call your mother."

Wade smirked. Jessa caught the look and moved back toward the suitcase.

She muttered to herself, "Everyone in that hospital was judging me. So, I left."

Wade scoffed.

"Don't be ridiculous," he said.

"Everyone in that hospital is friends with your damn mother," she said. "They all just glare at me. Unlike you, they never fucking left me alone."

"You sound so fucking paranoid."

"I told them all to go to hell," Jessa said.

"You mean your dad's house?" Wade asked.

"Enough," she said to him. "I've had enough of you. And this entire day. Baby gets locked in a car, then hit by broken glass. I'm in a towel out on the damn lawn. I have to take the baby to the fucking hospital all goddamn day, and now you have decided you want to be here for the baby, now that I'm taking her away. And you blame me for all of this! Bullshit. I'm out."

"Not with my baby. You can leave."

"I have the breasts, Wade. I can take my baby wherever I want. Or don't you want your daughter to eat?"

Wade spat, "I'm glad your breasts are good enough for someone."

Her face turned scarlet. Jessa zipped the suitcase. Her father continued to pound at the door, so she waved at him through the window to indicate they were coming.

The suitcase went from the mattress to the ground. She extended its handle and wheeled it toward the door, baby in her other arm.

"We'll be back tomorrow for the rest of my stuff," she said to him, crossing the room. "Answer your fucking phone when I call."

Then, reaching the door, Jessa turned and said her exit line, like the whole thing was a drama.

"You're a terrible father," she said to him. The baby continued to cry. As she unlocked the door, Wade tried to reply to her honestly.

"We're both terrible." And then he threw his busted-screen phone at her like a rock. It zoomed past her and smacked the door with a crack, then bounced back to the floor.

She smirked at him, like it was all some joke, then opened the door. Rev. Lancaster—glaring at Wade, never speaking but never blinking—grabbed the suitcase so that its wheels wouldn't drag on the lawn.

Though tempted to chase both of the smug Lancasters down and beat them to death, Wade hesitated. There were too many witnesses. They'd never let him keep the baby. He didn't have a weapon. He didn't really want to be a killer. He didn't want his daughter to hate him. He didn't want his daughter to never know him. And, the thing that made him angriest, he feared Jessa was right.

CHAPTER TWENTY-TWO

WHEN CELESTE WAS GROWING UP, HER MOTHER USED TO FRET END-
LESSLY ABOUT HOW THE GIRL SPENT HER FREE TIME.

She'd eye the Lois Duncan and Stephen King books
warily, as though they were weapons or, worse, ciga-
rettes. The VHS copies of "A Nightmare on Elm Street"
and "Jagged Edge" troubled her so much that she
wouldn't even read the plot descriptions. Celeste spent
her evenings glued to cop shows, murder mysteries and
Lifetime movies.

"Looking at all that stuff is going to warp you," Mama
would say. "No wonder you're depressed. All that violence and sadness."

Celeste didn't think there was any danger in stories
warping her any more than the world itself would, same
as it does to everyone. But Mama didn't want to hear
any arguments. She would just worry that her daughter
wasn't "normal."

Mama spent her nights reading Harlequin romance
novels filled with happy endings and great kisses, Celeste thought, but those books never taught her mother
how to pick a good man. So there.

Celeste believed that violence in media didn't create a
violent, abusive or sad world. It just reflected it back. And
Celeste was fascinated by the darkness of the world, the
secrets that "normal" people had to hide. Thus, she took

it all in, the shows and the books and the movies. She found it an easy way to experience situations and relate to feelings without having to actually suffer through them. Stories teach compassion, Celeste learned. But her mama wouldn't hear it. Reading anything darker than Nancy Drew was going to ruin her.

"Good girls don't spend their time studying these monsters," Mama would lecture, which would just cause Celeste to turn up the volume on "Cagney and Lacey."

If what her mother believed was true, Celeste had been preparing to kill a man since middle school.

Sitting in Max's hospital room, staring at him as he writhed and muttered, Celeste wondered if she could actually kill a man, if it came down to it. She wondered if she could commit a perfect murder, if the media had taught her any way to get away with it.

The way Max was now, Celeste could easily off him, damn the consequences. She could just take his pillow or the plastic bag she'd carried out from Waffle House to smother him. She considered the irony of smothering someone with a bag that had carried Waffle House hash browns and smiled. Even Max would've appreciated that joke, she thought. Hash browns all-the-way were his cheat carb.

But Celeste couldn't kill Max, even if she knew he wasn't a good guy. Even if she knew Wade wasn't the first teenager he'd seduced. There were too many variables to consider, too many strings attached. Celeste had Marcus to think about. He was her priority.

Killing Max would not only endanger Celeste's life and freedom, it would also put a serious crimp in her job security. Keeping Max's office meant keeping Max's secrets, and Max paid her too well to keep those. She knew all his little habits. She knew the times he "accidentally" went into some irritating bitch's mouth when she wasn't numb enough. Celeste knew when he'd take his opportunity to "check out" the abs on some unconscious basketball star getting a root canal. Max was loose about ethics, but Celeste understood what motivated him. He took out his grievances while helping people at the same time, he told her. And that made it OK.

"If I help someone, what does it matter how I help someone?" he asked her when she complained, early in their working relationship, maybe three years ago.

Celeste kept her mouth shut and kept cashing checks. And she kept her son fed, clothed, housed and in a good school. All the money she saved for Marcus. He was going to be better than everybody, better than some deadbeat dad, better than some dental assistant, better than some jackass dentist. The world wasn't going to warp her son. Marcus would be well-equipped. He knew he was loved and supported. And her son read James Baldwin, Time Magazine, poetry and science books.

In spite of herself, Celeste liked Max too much to personally kill him. She liked his jokes. It's hard to murder someone who makes you laugh, even if this whole town would be better off if Max never left this room again.

"Damn you for being nice to me, you son of a bitch," she said to him as he rested, all bandaged, sunken-eyed and pathetic.

Instead of murdering her boss, Celeste began un-packing all of the waffles she'd bought. She opened the door to his hospital room, letting the smell of fresh baked treats waft out into the hallway while they were still warm. After that was done, she unpacked the marked-down Whitman's Samplers and Hershey's Kisses she'd bought from the hospital drugstore. Celeste knew—from all her mother's surgeries years back—that patients with food got the best attention.

And Celeste wanted one nurse on Eight West in particular to come by Max's room an awful lot. Celeste thought she and Mary Harrell might have a lot to discuss once they got to know each other.

The waffles got Mary to the door, chart in hand, hun-ger in her eyes, within two minutes. "This is my last stop of the night," she explained. "I'm just checking in."

Noting the hunger in the nurse's eyes, Celeste smiled, gestured toward the other chair in the room and said, "Have a seat."

Twenty minutes later, the last crumbs of Mary's waffle soaked in syrup on the adjustable tray, and the nurse and the dental assistant gabbed like friends, wash-ing down the food with miniature cans of ginger ale snagged from the dining cart.

"You think Max is going to make it out of this all right?" Celeste asked.

"He's not out of the woods yet, but it's good that he woke up once already," Mary said. "The next few days are key."

Celeste shook her head in pity.

"How long have you worked with him?" Mary asked.

"It feels like forever," Celeste said. "But I guess it's been several years now, ever since his last assistant just walked out without warning."

"That sounds like a story," Mary said.

"Whatever she saw couldn't have been nearly as bad as walking in on him lying face down in a pool of blood this morning," Celeste said. "I can tell you that right now."

"Yeah, that's going to be a hard sight to forget," Mary said. "What do you think happened?"

"He slipped and hit his head on the marble countertop, I think," Celeste lied.

"Jesus," Mary spat. "That'd have to be a pretty bad fall. I thought maybe somebody didn't like their bill."

Celeste tried to laugh it off.

"I mean, he's not the best guy sometimes, honestly," Celeste said. "But that whole sight was just scary as fuck."

Mary nodded.

"Sorry for my language."

"Oh please, I've heard it," Mary said. "I have a teenager."

"I know," Celeste said. "So do I."

"Oh really? How old?"

"Marcus is 14, going on 30," Celeste said.

"You have no idea how much I relate," Mary said, smirking. "My boy's already made me a grandmother."

"You don't look like a grandmother," Celeste admitted.

"I shouldn't be one yet," Mary said. "But I shouldn't be a widow either."

Mary's voice trailed off, then she sighed a moment. Trying to compose herself, she muttered, "At least Lydie is cute."

Celeste touched Mary on the hand.

"It sounds tough," Celeste said. "I know raising a boy on your own is hard. I can't imagine if Marcus was a daddy."

Mary tried to compose herself, though she felt like crying. She took a sip of ginger ale. It was too much.

"Wade's life is so complicated," Mary said. "I never wanted that for him. But he had to grow up quick. And I don't know what's going through his head most of the time. I swear, today was the first time we'd had a real conversation, and I don't even know where that came from."

"Wade's life *is* complicated," Celeste agreed.

"Hmm?" Mary said, puzzled that this woman would know much of anything about Wade.

"Oh, I've met your son, remember?"

"Oh right, Wade was in the hallway with you this afternoon," the nurse remembered. Celeste's eyes bugged a little bit.

"That wasn't the first time I met Wade," Celeste said. "Or you. You don't remember me driving him home from our office after that surgery?"

"You did what?"

"We called you from the office to see if you could pick him up," Celeste explained. "But you were stuck at the hospital. I just drove him to your house and left him with that girl and her baby."

Mary rolled her eyes at the mention of Jessa.

178

"That girl just put him under a blanket, probably, and went back to watching TV," Mary said.

"Yeah," Celeste said. "She wasn't much from the looks of her."

"How do you remember all this stuff, Celeste?"

"I just have one of those brains," the assistant said.

Mary shivered and said, "Sorry. I meet so many patients myself. I just figured it was the same way with you, that you wouldn't remember everybody, even after a couple months."

"Oh, Wade was memorable," Celeste said. "I think I still have the video from that car ride on my phone."

"WHAT? YOU'RE KIDDING ME."

"Oh yeah, he was babbling from the painkillers," she confessed. "I couldn't help but film him. Boy was hilarious. Zonked out like a baby but talking about the craziest stuff like Elmer Fudd."

Mary laughed, then said, "You know I have to see it now, right?"

Celeste knew. Celeste knew all too well that Mary needed to see it. It's what NancyDrew would have done.

Celeste pulled up the video on her phone, leaned it against the ice pitcher in front of Mary and pressed Play.

Δ

The video opened on Wade, slouched and sleepy-eyed in the backseat of his own car. The baby seat was next to him. He petted it like a cat while he looked out the window. He drooled.

"What you were saying about the dentist?" Celeste said in the recording, snickering.

"*Doctowww Emmetttt isss beauwwwtifuwww, and I wanna smooooooch his face,*" Wade said, his mouth all amush. "*Daaaah dennisssss. Daaaaaaaaaah. Dennissssss. Whooooo arrrrre youuuuuu? Whewwwe awww weeee? Your bwwwwaids are pwwwweeeeetttty.*"

"I'm his assistant," Celeste told Wade. "I'm driving you back home."

At this, Wade dozed off for a moment, then roused himself.

"*Whooooo are youuuu?*" he asked again.

"Honey, keep talking," Celeste said. "You're hilarious."

"*Whooo are youuuuu? Isss thiss really happeningggg?*"

"We're going to put this on YouTube," she said to him. "I'm driving you home. This shit is gold, baby."

"*Whaaaat? WHOO ARE YOOOOOU?*"

The nav system spoke up, telling Celeste that she was approaching the house. Wade looked puzzled, confused and scared. He started crying.

The video ended abruptly.

Δ

Celeste turned to Mary as it ended. As Celeste suspected, the nurse was not laughing at all. Instead, her face was white. Mary looked at the dentist, alarmed.

"What?" Celeste asked her.

"Huh," Mary said. "I've never found Dr. Emmett that beautiful."

Celeste smirked, "Especially not now."

Mary took a breath.

"I wish I'd seen that video months ago," she admitted, turning to Celeste. "It would've made today's conversation with Wade so much easier."

Celeste confessed, "Dr. Emmett told me not to show that video to anyone after he saw it."

"He saw it?"

"Oh yeah," Celeste admitted. "I thought he'd find it funny. But instead he went to talk to Wade about it."

"What are you talking about? Why would he talk to my son?" Mary asked.

"I thought you knew about all this," Celeste said.

"Dr. Emmett came to my house? Wade never said anything about that."

"Nah, he talks to Wade at the grocery store," Celeste said in a deadpan voice, careful at how she tossed the metaphorical grenade. "Max shops there almost every night."

At that admission, Mary's eyes fixed upon the dentist and would not leave him. Her eyes grew wider and wider. Celeste watched the nurse, saying no more about it.

CHAPTER TWENTY-THREE

MARY WANTED TO CALM HERSELF ON HER DRIVE HOME. She wanted to just zone out and relax a little bit before she con-
fronted Wade at the house, assuming he was there. But
the double assault of Thursday night rush hour traffic
in suburban Atlanta and the radio inexplicably blasting
"I'm Gonna Be (500 Miles)" by The Proclaimers within
moments of her car starting made her feel like she was
in a hostage situation. Mary changed the radio station to
NPR, hoping for calm voices, but it was all Trump news
and, worse, the fundraising campaign where they asked
you to donate your car for some reason.

That fucking dentist molested her goddamn son.
Fucking fuck, that piece of shit. And his damn nurse just
casually mentioned it to her over waffles, for Christ's
sake. And Wade didn't even fucking tell her any of this.
He just stood there in the hallway of the hospital, staring
at the dentist, and he told her nothing.

And since he's a goddamn teenager, he won't get
why holding back such things is akin to lying to her face.
He will act like he was just trying to spare her feelings
or whatever, just like he did when he got Jessa pregnant.

Mary found out that her son had gotten a girl pregnant from the girl's father, for fuck's sake. That minister
emailed Mary, saying that her son had ruined his pre-
cious angel or some bullshit. Last summer, Mary opened

her Gmail to find some email from Rev. Lancaster she thought was spam, until she saw the subject line was "What Wade did."

And now Mary found herself wondering, again, what Wade has been doing. School suspension. Sexual confusion. Teen pregnancy. Visiting some comatose child-molesting motherfucker's hospital room.

What the hell kind of Thursday was this? Like, seriously.

To herself, aloud, Mary asked, "How the hell is this my life?"

The radio just replied with the broken staccato voice of arts journalist Lois Reitzes, describing what was going to happen on the next episode of "City Lights."

Mary switched off the radio, praying that the silence was more calming.

Instead, she was just trapped in her car, staring at all the idiots on the road, lost in occasional thoughts of some dentist drilling her son's mouth. It took her 45 minutes to drive eight miles.

When the driveway came into sight, she realized that she was eager to get home and also in no real hurry to have any of her suspicions confirmed. She had all the questions she could consider, yet she dreaded getting any answers.

Wade's Prius was in the driveway, the back window covered with a cardboard box. Mary almost regretted ever having children at the sight of it.

She stepped out of her Yaris. And, almost immediately, that nosy bitch Mrs. Winston's front door opened, and the lady was waving her down. Mary ignored her, which just brought her further out of the house.

"Mrs. Harrell, this place has been like Grand Central Station today," the neighbor said. "And your son was absolutely awful to me."

Mary glared at Mrs. Winston and muttered, "Get away from me and my driveway, Flo." Mrs. Winston ignored this and just kept saying how much of a terror Wade was.

"He doesn't have to be nice to you, lady," Mary said. "Particularly when you smash the windows out of his car, which, by the way, you're going to pay for."

The lady approached further.

"Stay off of my driveway," Mary said. "You aren't welcome here ever again."

"I was trying to save the baby," Mrs. Winston said calmly.

"Bullshit," Mary said. "If you were at all interested in the baby, you would've gotten my son first. You wouldn't have scared the baby and shattered broken glass all over her. You would've knocked on our door. I know you saw where he went. You're always watching."

"But—"

"If you think you're a help to anyone with all the crap you pull, Flo, then you must be deluded," Mary said to the woman, who started to retreat back toward her own house. "No wonder your husband left you."

At that, Mrs. Winston turned tail and ran.

"I know exactly who you are," Mary spat at the woman. "You're fooling no one, you miserable bitch."

Mary inhaled, exhaled and then prepared for her next battle. She walked up on to the porch of her house, walked through the front door and expected to see Wade in her living room. Mary assumed his mess would be dropped at her feet whenever it was too big for him, like a science fair project that he forgot to do. But Wade was not in her living room. So, instead, Mary headed to the kitchen.

She approached the faucet and turned on the tap. The water ran with a whoosh, just loud enough. She foisted herself up on the counter next to it, pulled herself up by the refrigerator and stared at the closed cabinet door. Whatever Wade's secrets, love notes or whatever, she would find them there. She opened the door, expecting something benign like papers or receipts.

Instead, she saw a gleaming model set of braces, teeth and gums. She reached for it, pulling the model out. It had a weight to it, like a couple stacked coffee cups. Mary looked even closer at the braces, noticing only the slightest hint of blood.

Suddenly, Wade's voice spoke up, watching her from the basement door. She didn't know how long he had been standing there.

"Mom—," he said meekly, looking up at her on the counter. And she saw fear more than confusion in his eyes.

CHAPTER TWENTY-FOUR

WADE'S MOTHER HELD THE TEETH IN HER HAND. His daughter was gone, and Jessa had no intention of coming back. His lover had become his victim. He knew what it was to murder someone, even if he hadn't actually done that. He knew he was capable of it. Wade knew he deserved to suffer for what he'd done. He knew his life was over, that all was lost. He wanted to die. He'd rather die. He didn't want his mom to hate him. Mary was looking at him, then looking at the teeth. She was confused and angry.

Still, she'd gone right to the cabinet. She hadn't hesitated. He saw her. She knew to look for something. She knew where he hid things. She looked at him like she knew everything, even though she couldn't possibly know, short of Dr. Emmett waking up and telling her about it. He knew instinctively that wasn't the case. But Wade didn't know what the case was.

Wade didn't want his mom to hate him. He wanted her to know his secrets and not hate him. He couldn't read her face completely. He couldn't figure out how to even start talking.

He looked up at her, awkwardly contorted over the refrigerator, and he said, "Mom—," before he had any clue how to fill out the rest of the sentence.

She turned to him and just said, "Yes," like there wasn't a chasm of emotion separating them. She held the jaw, her fingers ran along the braces, and Wade started to stammer to her, hoping that somehow the words would make better sense once they left him and entered the air between them.

"Mom, I just—"

"What, Wade?"

Her voice was as cold as he imagined February was supposed to be. He shivered.

"I just wanted to—"

"You need to say a lot of things, Wade," she said to her son. "It's better if you don't hesitate."

"But, Mommy, I—"

"'*Mommy*'? Don't."

"Mom, what?"

"You aren't a baby, Wade. Don't 'Mommy' me. Just say what you want me to hear."

"I don't know what you want to hear."

"Just start somewhere."

Mary maneuvered herself to her knees to put the jaw on the counter, then she scooched herself back on to the ground. She was older now, it wasn't graceful. He remembered when she was young, how smoothly she used to move. He believed his parents could do anything when he was a kid. His mom and dad were such heroes. No one could defeat them. Wade didn't want his mom to hate him. He wanted to die.

"Just start somewhere because I don't know what I want to hear, either," Mary said.

"Did Dr. Emmett wake up?" Wade asked.

"No."

"Is he dead?"

"Not so far."

"Cool," Wade said for some idiotic reason that made him hate himself.

"Tell me how you know him."

"He's my dentist."

Her eyes bugged out. "Wade, I swear to God—"

"OK, he's my friend."

"What kind of friend, Wade? Talking to you is like pulling teeth."

She probably said it unintentionally. Wade glanced at the jaw. She kept her eyes laser-focused on his. His stomach tightened. He wanted to disintegrate.

"Just say it, Wade."

"How do you know?"

"Say it, Wade."

"I don't want to tell you."

"Are you in love with him, Wade?"

A beat.

"No."

His mother lifted an eyebrow, then muttered, "Good. At least there's that." She said it like she hated him.

"Mom, I'm sorry," Wade said.

"For what, exactly? Use sentences."

"Please don't be mean," he said.

"You're not a toddler, Wade. You made choices not to tell me things. I don't know what the hell this—*what is it?*—mouth is, and I'm freaking out because I'm going crazy trying to figure out an explanation for any of this. I don't know why you didn't tell me that your dentist was chit-chatting with you every night at work. I'm not mean. I want to know what you have been doing. I want to know what you were doing with my patient today. I want to know what you were doing every night while I watched your baby and put up with your girlfriend's crap. I want to know right now."

His face turned white. Then, he recovered his gumption.

"You don't need to worry about the girlfriend anymore. She's gone."

"Don't change the subject, Wade. Tell me everything about Dr. Emmett."

"How do you know about this stuff if he didn't wake up?"

"Now, damn it!" she shouted. "Don't stall. Don't ask questions. Your dentist has been fucking you. Don't make me guess anymore."

"Mom—"

"I know you don't want to tell me, that much is abundantly clear, but, Wade, the only way you and I get through this situation is straight through it."

With that, Wade sat down at the kitchen table, opened the door to the story and promised to tell his mother the truth. Though he didn't like her touching it, Mary carried the tooth model to the table and sat it on the Formica between them.

Δ

"Dr. Emmett would show up when I was restocking the cereal aisle around 11. He must've asked someone for my schedule, I don't know. At first, I thought it was just a coincidence, that he just really, really ate a lot of fiber or something. It didn't occur to me that he was coming to see me."

"When was this?" Mary asked him.

"Just a week or so after I had that wisdom tooth removed."

"That didn't seem weird to you?"

"It's a small town, Mom. I don't know. I see teachers at the store all the time. I don't think they come in to see me."

"But he talked to you every night? For how long, Wade?"

"It was a couple weeks, I think," he said. "I wasn't really getting any sleep then. It was a blur. You remember?"

"I remember thinking you hated the baby," Mary admitted. "Or that you were the slowest damn stock boy in the world."

Wade chuckled. But she wasn't having it. There was no calming down, no joking anymore. He thought she hated him. He wanted to die.

"Tell me about the dentist."

"What about him?"

"Tell me who he is."

"Huh?"

"You're not this dumb, Wade. Stop acting like you don't know what I mean. Tell me about this man. Tell me about your friendship."

"I get that," Wade said to his mother. "It's just not easy."

"It won't get any easier. Tell me."

"Dr. Emmett said he got lonely at home by himself, that he got bored watching TV. He said he missed living in a city, like the ones in the wallpaper on his office. He said he was a night-owl, and he liked talking to people like me."

"People like you?"

"Dr. Emmett said bartenders and waitresses and bagboys had the best stories. He said they saw all kinds of people, usually at their worst. He said he liked how colorful people can be when they're doing boring, mundane shit. He asked me if I paid attention to people."

"And do you?"

"I don't know. I guess. Like, he asked me if anybody ever hummed to themselves, not noticing or ignoring that I was in the aisle."

"Why would he ask that?"

"Not just about that, but, like, anything," Wade said. "That first night, I told him that people sometimes would dance around to the Muzak. And that couples would just argue sometimes, right there in the freezer section, over ice cream."

"Like, you mean, what flavor?"

"No, there was a legit fight about whether a guy's suggestion of ice cream was a passive-aggressive dig at his girlfriend."

Mary snickered.

"Dr. Emmett just seemed nice, Mom," Wade said. "He asked about the baby and Jessa and my tooth. He asked me about Christmas and stuff."

"And what did you say to him?"

"That the baby was new and scared the hell out of me. And that I was tired all the time."

"And about Jessa?"

"I said that, since we had Lydie around, Jessa didn't care whether I existed. And he—"

"What?"

"He told me that I did exist, that he saw me," Wade said. "People shopping for egg nog and Christmas cookies might ignore me. The girl in my basement might not acknowledge me. You might be too mad to look at me. But Dr. Emmett said he saw me."

"When was I too mad to look at you?" Mary asked.

"Oh, come on, Mom, you can't stand me," Wade said. "I disappoint you all the time. I disappointed you in May when I didn't tell you Jessa was pregnant. I annoyed you to death when the baby was born. You acted like I didn't know how to do anything."

"Well, you didn't," she said.

"So? You didn't have to be so mean about it," Wade said. "You probably didn't know how to handle a baby 'til you had me."

"You need a thicker skin if that got to you," she said. "Jesus, I thought you were tougher than that."

"You treat me like I'm an idiot," Wade said.

"Well, sometimes you're an idiot, damn it."

Wade shook his head.

"Yeah, but I can't be doing everything wrong all the time, right?" Wade asked. "Why do you all act like I can't do anything right ever? It irritates the fuck out of me.

You think I'm a jerk. Jessa thinks I ignore her. I can't do anything right with the baby. I am always in trouble at work. But I can't figure out how to fix it. Like, was I always a loser? Is everything my fault? How is that even possible?"

Wade was red in the face. Mary's eyes widened.

"Um, don't be ridiculous. Let's get back to talking about the dentist."

"No, you need to listen to me first. Why am I a worthless piece of shit all the time?"

"When have I ever called you that or treated you like that? I never use that kind of language, first of all."

Wade rolled his eyes at that one.

"Please, Mom," he scoffed. "I live here. I know you."

"I don't treat you like that," she affirmed.

"You might not think you do, but that's how I feel all the time."

"Don't be melodramatic, Wade."

"All. The. Time. I feel like that all the time. Listen to me." Mary paused.

Wade looked her in the eye, holding her attention.

"I need you to hear me. I've been going over how all this happened in my head."

"How you were molested by some 35-year-old predator who groomed you?" she asked. "Is that what you mean 'happened'? Because, Wade, that's what happened."

"That isn't what it seemed like, Mom," he said.

"Wade, he tracked you down."

"To be nice to me."

"And then, let me guess, he kept coming back."

"Yeah, I guess, but—"

"And the conversations got so long and so deep that he suggested y'all talk after your shift."

"Yeah."

"And he bought you beer or wine or something, and he asked you to share it," she continued.

"Who told you this?"

"And you felt light-headed, and he started to touch you. And then things were weird."

"Mom, I wasn't powerless."

"You were a child, Wade," she said. "You were a child that he drugged and touched."

"It wasn't like that! I was talking to him, and he was nice to me, and it just happened," Wade said with a raised voice. "And I can make my own choices."

"This isn't your fault, Wade," she said.

"He didn't make me—"

"Did you start it? Did you suggest it?"

"I told him that he was hot, I said it over and over."

"When you were sedated," Mary clarified.

"How do you know about this?"

"Did you initiate sex with your dentist?"

"Well, no, but—" Wade stammered, feeling out of control.

"Because he molested you."

"I don't know," Wade said. "I feel like this is all my fault."

"So, do lots of people who are molested, son," she said. "When they're vulnerable, someone takes advantage of them, then initiates them into keeping a secret. And you feel out of control. And lost. And angry at yourself. I'm sorry that this happened to you."

He felt like she didn't get it.

"It wasn't like that—"

"It was, Wade. Dr. Emmett's not a good guy."

"But, Mom, he was nice—"

"Nice and good aren't the same."

"I don't think I'm some victim."

"I understand how that can happen, son."

"I told him to do it," Wade said. "I pushed his head down."

"His head was already on the way, probably."

"Well, we went away—"

"And you were too young."

"Mom, stop it," Wade said, for she couldn't be right about this. He wasn't a child. He wasn't attacked. Those things look different than what happened to him, and he couldn't figure out how to make her see what he chose to happen.

"You were too young to choose anything," she said, as though finishing his thought.

His mind was racing, confused. Her version of events wasn't wrong, but it wasn't how he wanted to see himself. It wasn't right. He didn't want to be powerless in every aspect of his life. He didn't want to be someone everyone decided things for. Wade didn't want to be a victim. She kept acting like they were in this together, like he needed help. She acted like none of the mistakes were his, that none of the choices were his. Wade didn't feel innocent.

He didn't want to be used. He was angry. And his mommy was coming in like she was going to save him from a predator. But he'd already saved himself.

Mary just kept telling him it wasn't his doing.

"I hit him, Mom!" Wade shouted angrily, his eyes moving from that damned mouth to her. He pushed his chair back, lifted the Formica table off the floor and then slammed it on the ground. The teeth slid toward him, and he stared at them, continuing to rant at his mother.

"Since you think you know everything about what happened with Dr. Emmett! Do you know that much, huh? *Do you know that I hit him in the head?!*"

CHAPTER TWENTY-FIVE

WADE'S PHONE VIBRATED IN HIS POCKET, BLESSEDLY INTERRUPTING HIS TALK WITH HIS MOTHER AFTER OVER AN HOUR OF BACK-AND-FORTH DEBATE. After that long, going over what he'd done as specifically as he could recall, the boy had reached his limit. Her stance was unchanged, so far as Wade could tell. He was merely the victim in all this, even when he attacked Dr. Emmett, according to her.

"He was a child-molesting pervert son of a bitch, Wade," his mother said, hitting her same notes over and over. "You should've gone ahead and killed him. And you should've done it months ago."

His eyes widened toward her, unsure whether to find her scary ranting an endearing display of supportive motherhood. He didn't understand her take on this, for it wasn't how everything with the dentist during the past two months had happened. And he knew how the two months had gone. Because, unlike her, he'd been there when the relationship happened. Often without pants on. In Wade's mind, there was no escaping death by lethal injection.

The phone vibrated again.

He looked down at the number, then turned back toward his mom.

"It's the store," he lied to her. "I must've missed my shift."

"Wade, just ignore—" Mary started.

He put the phone to his ear and bolted from the table toward the basement, shutting the door behind him. His tell-all moment with his mother was over, and it would not start up again tonight.

"Trevor?" he asked into the receiver.

"Hi there," the cheery guy replied.

"Dude, you just saved my life."

"Huh?"

"You just saved me from the world's longest bad conversation." Wade walked down the steps and flopped down on the mattress.

"I was wondering if you wanted to grab that coffee early," Trevor asked him. "It's been the most hellish day."

Wade smiled at this and said, "You're telling me."

Δ

Forty-five minutes later, Wade sat in downtown Waverly at Happy Donuts, watching out the window for Trevor to arrive. For two days, the guy managed to show up un-expectedly in inconvenient places. Now, with a planned meeting, Wade found it sort of amusing that Trevor was running late. Wade found Trevor to be an interesting, quirky question mark, and he didn't seem to pose much of a threat to Wade—because Trevor didn't know what Trevor didn't know. Maybe this could be a positive. A friendship or a rare decent relationship, instead of a shit-show. Wade sat at his favorite coffee place and dared to hope.

Wade reconsidered himself, sitting there in a welcome moment of chill. *Am I gay?* he wondered. *Does this mean I'm gay?*

He considered the parts of the question. The literal parts involved in the question.

Wade thought about the back of Jessa's neck when they would lie together in bed, the strawberry scent in her hair, the shape of her body.

He thought of Dr. Emmett, the feel of his mouth, the intensity of passion.

Wade took a breath. Some questions didn't need an answer. His body chose both, so he guessed his feelings did too.

This was not the moment for a first date, yet a first date had presented itself. Wade longed for the escape. It spared him from having to think about Lydie and custody or his mother and her rantings or the dentist in his hospital bed, his head wrapped in bandages, his mind in some haze. Wade tried not to think on how much of a threat the man would pose to him once he was out of the hospital.

Dr. Emmett was going to cost Wade everything. The fear was familiar, echoing since December, but it carried more layers now.

Wade pictured Dr. Emmett getting wheeled out of the hospital by his mother, of all people, and taking an Uber straight to the police station. Wade imagined himself being tried as an adult for assault, getting his GED in prison, seeing Lydie only on sporadic weekends until she turned 20. Wade imagined the names that Rev. Lancaster would tell Lydie to call him once the truth came out, the sort of words you wouldn't expect a minister to say. Yet Wade imagined them coming all too easily from Rev. Lancaster about the boy who "ruined his daughter."

Wade imagined Dr. Emmett finding some new young man in his chair, how Celeste would roll her eyes at the seduction all over again but wouldn't stop it. She'd just keep cashing paychecks and minding her business, Wade figured. The new boy would be better than Wade, less needy and better at keeping a secret. The new boy would drive some electric car, even quieter than a Prius, and Dr. Emmett would take advantage of that at every opportunity. Dr. Emmett would seduce the new one, then belittle him, then ignore him, then bring him back. Dr. Emmett would take. He would give nothing. He would manipulate someone new, and he'd be better at it while Wade rotted away in some cell.

Δ

When a cleaned-up and shiny Trevor walked into the donut shop five minutes late, muttering apologies, Wade heaved uncomfortable, unexpected sobs.

"What is it? What's up?" Trevor asked Wade, genuinely concerned. "I'm so sorry I was late. I couldn't pick the right shirt."

Wade wiped his eyes with a napkin but could not easily speak. "I just—"

"Did something happen?"

"My life, I'm sorry, my life is such a mess," Wade said.

"Did something happen with your dad?"

"What?" Wade asked, confused. "My dad?"

"Do you need to go back to the hospital?"

"No," Wade said emphatically. "Hell no."

Trevor looked at Wade, trying to read the situation, but Wade could see that he'd bewildered his date.

"Wade, do you want to talk about what happened just now?" Trevor asked. "You said you'd had a bad day."

"No," Wade replied. "Tell me about your day."

Wade didn't want to think about himself. He didn't want to tell this new person about his girlfriend. Or their baby. He especially didn't want to tell him anything about his "dad."

"So, like, it's almost every morning that they bug me one way or another," Trevor explained, ripping apart an Oreo doughnut in his hand. "I can handle myself, but some days you just don't feel like fighting, you know? I'm gonna quit eventually. But it pays better than working at some restaurant, right?"

"Sure," Wade said, intently watching this guy's manner. His hands would flit. He'd toss his hair. His eyes would sparkle as he talked. And he talked fast, excited for the next words to come out, even if they were about how his co-workers knocked him around. Trevor moved with grace, his voice carried a note of confidence, and no part of him seemed to be hiding. Wade envied that.

"I've been fighting all my life, it feels like. From the time I was a kid, my dad would try and make me into somebody I'm just not. Like, he would take me to the pool during each weekend he had custody."

"Your parents are divorced?"

"Not now," Trevor said. "Now, they're married to other people. But they're divorced from each other, if that's what you mean. My brother and I used to shuttle between Mom's house and Dad's house every other weekend. Dad lived in this apartment complex up around Sandy Springs. You ever get up there?"

"Not really."

"I swear, every divorced dad in the metro area moves to Sandy Springs, it's kind of ridiculous," Trevor said. "Anyway, so Dad was always trying to get me to be more athletic and stuff. But I would only do sports that he wouldn't be remotely interested in. I took dance classes, which is why my ass looks like this now."

"What?" Wade asked.

"Oh," Trevor smiled. "I was just checking to see if you were paying attention. Am I talking too much? I know I can just go on."

Wade looked at Trevor, attempted a reassuring nod like the kind he'd seen in the movies. He'd never been through something that felt like this before. Most of his dates with Dr. Emmett, the two of them never left the Prius.

"You can talk as much as you like, Trevor," Wade said. "This is the most fun I've had all day."

"Then you must not masturbate as much as I do," Trevor replied. At that, Wade turned a bit red.

"Gotcha," Trevor said with a smile. "So, tell me what your days are like?"

"Um," Wade muttered, "we don't need to talk about me."

"Go on, dude. You're safe with me. What, do you still live with your parents? How old are you again?"

"17."

"So, you're what, a senior?"

"No, a junior. I just turned 17, like, last week."

"I remember."

"Am I too young for you?"

"For this conversation, you mean?" Trevor asked. "I don't card people."

"No, I mean—"

"Wade, you don't have to be in a hurry," Trevor said. "We're just getting to know each other. And I think you're fine."

"Just fine?"

"Actually, I think you're really cute," Trevor smirked. "But that's all you'll get out of me. Keep talking."

"My living arrangement right now is a little bit wonky," Wade admitted. "I've lived in my mom's basement since December."

"Why the basement? Is it a *Flowers in the Attic* thing?"

"Huh?" Wade asked Trevor.

"Old book reference. Sorry."

"Oh."

"So, anyway, why do you live in your mom's basement? Are your parents divorced too?"

"Just since the baby," Wade said. "No, they aren't divorced."

"Your mom had a baby?"

"Nope, I did," Wade said.

"Ri-i-ight."

"I did," Wade explained, pulling out his phone and unlocking the front screen.

"Say what now?" Trevor asked.

Wade showed Trevor the photo on his background wallpaper, a shot of Lydie mesmerized by a mobile of giraffes and lions. "Her name is Lydie. She was born a couple days before Christmas. And Mom lets us stay in the basement."

"You and Lydie?"

"And Jessa, who is Lydie's mom."

Trevor looked baffled. "Wait, what?"

"This isn't going well, is it?"

"You have a live-in girlfriend and a baby, and you're only 17, living in your mom's basement?" Trevor asked.

"That's right," Wade said. "Is that a deal breaker?"

"It's different," Trevor said.

"Bad different?"

"It remains to be seen," Trevor said.

"I'd like to be seen," Wade said. "But I get that it's complicated."

He smiled and tried to pretend like he wasn't seriously crushing on Trevor, like he didn't care. Wade tried to make eye contact with Trevor.

And then Trevor asked something completely random, "Why do you keep calling it your mom's basement if they aren't divorced?"

"What do you mean?" Wade asked, taken aback. Trevor smirked.

"Your father's just in the hospital," Trevor said. "It's not like he's dead."

Wade smiled at the weird guy. Trevor's eyes widened at the smile but didn't return it. After that came the missed glances between each other, the random checking of the phone. Wade watched it all pass. He felt like he could've waved at it as it went by. The whole date ended after an hour with Wade suggesting that Trevor call him sometime.

"Sure," Trevor replied.

CHAPTER TWENTY-SIX

WADE STOOD AGAIN IN THE HOSPITAL ROOM ON EIGHT WEST AROUND 10 P.M. Dr. Emmett seemed to sleep so peacefully in his bed, his head wrapped in new and clean bandages, the sedatives working to keep him still.

The dentist's sound rest reminded Wade of their one night together, how they slept in each other's arms in that hotel, both of them spent from exertion, freshly showered. While Dr. Emmett dozed almost immediately upon hitting the pillow that night, Wade let himself live in the moment then. It seemed special at the time, weeks back. Wade felt loved then, sheltered and cared for by the dentist, even though *Leprechaun* had been playing during much of the passion.

Now, the boy felt like such a chump. His mother probably thought him some stupid, naive doormat who just let everyone wipe their feet on him. The voice inside his head just kept repeating "Stupid, stupid, stupid!" and no amount of singing any other tune would drown out that one.

He looked down at the dentist in his hospital bed. It made some weird sense to visit Dr. Emmett after that terrible date with Trevor. In a way, Dr. Emmett was Wade's only gay friend.

"Trevor's never going to talk to me again, Dr. Emmett," he said to his injured lover.

Wade knew that deep in his soul. Wade could always tell when someone was turned off by him—the kids at school, teachers who didn't like him, the neighbors. That sort of dislike felt fair to him, for he never found himself particularly likable either. He could never tell when someone liked him, the notion never occurred to him, that someone would look upon him and find him appealing.

Wade didn't think he was ugly, just that he was, like, there. Wade was the sort of background extra in every classroom, the kind of boy that blurred out of focus while the camera was rightfully directed at someone else.

Jessa didn't like him. Not really, Wade considered. She just went to him out of habit, because he was familiar.

Trevor shouldn't have liked him, Wade thought, and now he didn't.

And when Dr. Emmett liked him, apparently that wasn't real, Wade knew now.

Apparently, it was abuse that he was just the victim of, he was being conditioned and conned like a dolt. And Wade was dumb enough to think that it was love. Who could love him? He was a confused, clumsy child who made mistakes and giant messes. Everyone would be better off if Wade was just dead, maybe.

Maybe his dad would be there to say hello. Wade missed his dad. Maybe it would be safer there.

No. No, Wade thought. No. His own baby would never remember him. Lydie had a cute little face and her grandfather's eyes. And she had Wade's smile—when she had gas—and he couldn't leave her fatherless. He knew what that was like. Wade would not do that. Death like that was no answer, anyway.

Wade looked down at Dr. Emmett and remembered the dentist's bloody-eyed screaming. He remembered his own father's agony. He fixated on that terror. That was what death was like, pain and discomfort and blood and mess and wails that seemed to resonate from the heart and soul.

Wade had to save himself from even the smallest of those thoughts. He didn't want to die. He didn't want to die having made mostly mistakes. He didn't want to die because everything felt hopeless. He didn't want Trevor to think Wade killed himself over some silly awkwardness at the donut shop.

If you exit, you don't get to find out how the story ends, Wade thought. If you leave, you have no control over how you're seen. And so, Wade, wanting away from his thoughts, began to talk to the hospitalized man in front of him, who owed him a good listen, particularly after all those times making him wait in a damned Prius for hours and hours.

The ones who survive are the ones who talk about the bad stuff. Had his dad told him that?

"I told my mother about us," Wade said to Dr. Emmett. Then he added sarcastically, "I don't think she approves."

Wade laughed.

"OK, fine, I know she doesn't."

Wade moved to a chair at the foot of Dr. Emmett's bed and let his fingers run over the blankets covering the dentist's knee.

"Mom used to tell me that people talked to folks in comas to keep them connected to the world," Wade said. "I know I want to be connected to the world. I assume you might, too."

He stopped himself, then started again.

"OK, this is crazy," Wade said. "I'm just talking to myself. You're not even in a coma, you're sedated, and I'm just being dramatic."

He stopped again.

"You know I'm dramatic, right?"

Then, he laughed, considering the situation and Dr. Emmett's bandage. "I suppose you would."

Wade tried to think of the one thing he really wanted to say, if he had to boil it down. He couldn't stay here all night. One of the other nurses might tell his mom.

"Look, Max, I'm really sorry about yesterday, you just kind of pissed me off is all," Wade said. "Max, you treat me like shit, and I don't trust you at all. You aren't supposed to do the shit you do. Not to me or anyone. Ever."

Wade took a deep breath. It felt liberating to use the man's name. It put them on the same level. Wade always wanted to be more of a grown-up. He was always in such a hurry to know where he stood. He never thought of himself as a kid.

He thought about his car ride with Celeste. He considered his chat with his mom. Not even the grown-ups had the first idea of how to deal with this stuff.

"Celeste and my mom told me all about the way you pick up guys who are my age," Wade said to him. "Celeste even says you've done worse stuff. She says you seem to get off on it. Is that true, Max?"

Wade paused.

"I don't want to believe it," he explained. "I'd rather think that you're just a guy who liked me. And that you were nice enough to care. And that we had something special, even."

Wade started to tremble.

"I'd rather believe in goddamn Santa Claus and unicorns, too," Wade said. "But the world is more fucked up than that. It isn't romantic or cozy. It isn't even kind."

He stopped trembling.

"I don't know what the fuck you did to me or what it made me do to myself or think about myself," Wade said. "But it sure as fuck wasn't healthy or right."

The boy stood up.

"I can't be here anymore," Wade said. "Look, I'm gonna go. Thanks for the talk."

He held still, staring at the dentist, waiting for the man to wake up and maybe say goodbye. The dentist just continued sleeping soundly, his chest rising and falling. Wade left the room and walked back down the hallway of Eight West.

CHAPTER TWENTY-SEVEN

MARY MADE A POINT OF BEING IN HER BEDROOM WHEN WADE ARRIVED HOME. If he would rather run off than talk to her about how he attacked a child molester, for God's sake, she would leave him be about the situation for now. If he'd rather not talk about how he'd been keeping secrets from her for months, it upset her, but it made sense. Dark places aren't easy to dwell in. And if her son didn't want to talk about how his stupid girlfriend had left with their baby, Mary supposed she had no say in the matter. She was just a passenger on this ride while her son drove all of their lives off a cliff. But if he wanted to avoid talking about it for now, what else could Mary do?

Her son was sometimes so checked out. Other times, he was defensive, impulsive, violent, sad, funny and hurt. But Wade was never what she needed him to be when she needed him to be that. Without fail, he defied her, even if Mary thought she had better sense than her son about these things.

It made her fucking sick to think about it. How could she have been so blind? Lydie was distracting, certainly, constantly in need of food or holding or attention. But Mary felt like such a damned idiot for being so available to help her kid with one problem. All that did was free him up to cause or become involved in a whole set of new ones.

Wade was very much his father's son, Mary thought. Lydon went for days sometimes without telling her what the doctors were saying about his cancer. Because she was a nurse, Lydon would say he was sparing her. Her husband argued that she would always assume the worst, no matter what.

Really, all Lydon was doing was saving himself the grief, not her. Because she would've kept him healthier for longer. She would've nagged him until he was living as well as he could, a restricted diet, good exercise, the most aggressive medicines. Mary was a fighter. Mary was the best advocate for her patients.

They would argue about it in the beginning of the illness. Eventually, Lydon just yelled at her that he wanted a wife, not a nurse.

"I'm a wife, and I'm a nurse," Mary replied. "Damn it, Lydon."

"Mary, I just can't," Lydon said. "Let me just go."

By being good in one way, she wanted to be good in another. But Lydon didn't want every one of his waking moments to be some kind of fight, either with her or with the cancer. And so, he spent his time, sometimes, checking out, avoiding her, not having the deep, necessary conversations as soon as possible. He'd throw around words like "intense" and "insufferable," but Mary did keep him alive longer than the doctors said he had. And, in the end, Lydon thanked her for giving them time, even if he hated how she did it in the moments before.

Mary solved problems. People don't really tolerate problem solvers. They appreciate the end of the problems, but they don't like the process. Nobody buys champagne for their accountant with their tax refunds. They just show their appreciation by bringing back more receipts the next year.

Wade would never participate in the solutions, but her son would be grateful to her if she managed to clean up his mess.

With that in mind, she texted Stephanie at the hospital.

"If you need anyone to cover a shift tonight, let me know. Wake me up whenever. Jessa's been awful to Wade. I have got to get out of the house."

Within moments, Stephanie replied, "Will do. Jasmine wants to leave around 3 a.m., I think. Trying to catch her boyfriend cheating or something. That cool?"

"Hell yes," Mary replied.

She heard Wade shuffling around the kitchen, but she wouldn't give him the satisfaction of an acknowledgement. Mary slid her legs under the covers and turned off her lamp.

Laying in the dark, she wondered if Wade was anything like her, some way that she just couldn't see. At times, she could be angry or frustrated. At work, she would obsess over problems until they were done. And she didn't really have a lot of friends that she spoke to about anything, not in this town. For a little while after Lydon died, Mary had gone to see a therapist to talk through her grief. That had helped some. Mary still had that therapist's number in her phone.

That Celeste had been fun to talk with, maybe the two of them could've been friends under different circumstances, Mary thought. As it stood, Mary hoped to never see that woman ever again. Celeste had protected her own son and sacrificed Wade, in a way, to do that. Mary understood that. But Celeste could've taken care of the dentist in other ways.

To really help, Celeste could've exposed Dr. Emmett. But that would've cost her a paycheck. As a result, Mary's son suffered. And Mary's son fought to protect himself when no one else would help him. And now he was torturing himself over it. That made Mary's blood boil.

Δ

At 2:30 a.m., Mary's alarm went off. No need for a shower, she put on her scrubs quickly and headed downstairs to the kitchen. She grabbed a smoothie from out of the fridge, saw that the lights down in the basement were still on. Wade was still awake. Mary opened the door a crack, heard him rustling through some things. As the door opened, he stopped.

"Mom?" he asked her.

Mary hesitated and then replied, "I'm headed to work soon. What are you still doing up?"

"Packing up Jessa's shit," Wade muttered to himself more than to his mother, who didn't cross the threshold or go down the steps. "She said she'd come by and get it tomorrow, and I don't want her here any longer than necessary."

"Is she bringing the baby?"

"I assume," Wade said. "But I didn't ask her."

"She probably won't," Mary said from the top of the stairs. "She doesn't want any reason to stick around here, either. Besides, Mrs. Lancaster is probably having too much fun finally, finally acknowledging that she has a damn granddaughter."

"You and I are on the same page about that," Wade said to his mom, laughing.

Then, Mary had an idea.

"You know what, Wade?"

"What, Mom?"

"Leave that box for her on the front porch. Don't even bother to be here when she comes. She'll want a scene. Don't give that girl the satisfaction."

"Good idea," Wade said.

"When is she coming, anyway?" Mary asked.

"Probably after school or something," her son said.

Mary took a breath, then dared to breach the topic again with her son. She was not going to let him suffer.

"Wade, I'm going to set up an appointment for you to talk to someone," she said to him, taking full advantage of the fact that he couldn't argue with her as easily when they weren't face to face. "I'll text you details later. Try to get some sleep."

Then, as he started to ask her questions or bitch at her or object, Mary shut the door and then walked out her own front door to her car.

Mary clocked in at work at 3 a.m., then checked in with Stephanie.

She made small talk with her friend.

"I don't think Jessa's going to be a problem for Wade any longer," she told Stephanie. "When I left, he was packing her stuff up."

Stephanie sighed and said, "I did not like that girl. Was the baby OK?"

Mary paused, considering Lydie. "I never saw her, actually. But I assume I would hear something about it if there was trouble."

"You're probably right," Stephanie said.

"Those kids can't do anything without me," Mary said.

"I think all new parents are like that, though," Stephanie replied. "You're probably right."

Leaving Four West, Jasmine brushed past them both, thanking Mary for coming in early to cover and telling her that she'd not left anything pressing for Mary to do. Still, Mary went one round with Jasmine's patients, checking on their needs, but, at that hour, most of them were asleep. She checked charts and vitals, gave pain meds to one of the elderly women recovering from surgery. While going through the closet for that medication, Mary passed by the blood thinners, the unused syringes, the insulin supply, grabbing everything she needed for the rounds.

And when Mary got to Jasmine's patient nearest the elevator, a diabetic boy who'd just had his appendix removed who was out like a light, Mary left her cart for vitals outside his door. The hall was mostly empty. She walked toward the elevator at a regular pace, hands in her pockets.

Mary hit the button for 8. When the elevator doors opened, she stepped inside.

Arriving on her usual floor, she nodded at the folks manning the nursing station and, like it was no big deal because it was no big deal, she entered Max Emmett's hospital room, where he still slept soundly.

She wanted to talk to him, and she wanted to yell. She wanted to torture him slowly, pulling out his finger-nails. She wanted to cut off his dick, then shove it down his fucking throat. She wanted him to have kids so that she could track them down and hurt them in some way, just so he fucking knew what it goddamn felt like. She wanted to shout from the rooftops that the man in this bed, right here in this hospital, was a predator who hurt children and made them hate themselves. She wished her eyes could shoot lasers so that she could set him on fucking fire. She wanted to cry. She wanted to hit him. She wanted to stab him.

Instead, the expression was frozen on her face, the mood natural, the method completely professional. She injected three vials of insulin into his line. Then she pocketed the syringes, walked back into the hallway and pushed the button for the elevator again.

On the elevator, she took a deep breath. Returning to the fourth floor, Mary went back to her cart, then walked into the boy's room. In the medical waste there, she tossed the empty insulin packets and the syringes, where they wouldn't seem abnormal, just in case.

Nobody really monitored the insulin at Waverly General. Type-two diabetics were all too common. Since Max was already sedated, already expected to rest, no one would know or even think to check his blood sugar. If he became symptomatic from the hypoglycemia, his team would just treat him for the head injury. And, since Mary was on his medical team, she could assure it.

No one was asking questions. Nothing would seem abnormal.

He fell. He got a head injury. He never got completely better. These things were random. They just happen.

Dr. Emmett would never wake up again. In a couple of hours or days, he wouldn't be a problem for any of his patients—or their mothers—ever again. And perhaps no one would even miss him, Mary thought.

Mary continued working the shift like nothing was amiss. She wouldn't even permit herself a smile, even though the problem was solved. She wouldn't laugh about it, either, even if it was sort of poetic to have sugar kill a dentist.

CHAPTER TWENTY-EIGHT

THOUGH SHE WOKE UP AT 6:45 A.M., CELESTE PLANNED TO ARRIVE AT WORK AROUND 11:25 A.M. BECAUSE, HONESTLY, WHO WAS AROUND TO GIVE A SHIT? Seriously, she'd canceled all the appointments the day before, assuming Max would be incapacitated the rest of the week, at least, if not the weekend. Anybody who didn't check their messages would just arrive to a dark and locked office. And those people weren't worth her time.

Max's parents were flying in from Arizona that evening to check on him, the flights were all arranged. Their number was in his records. Celeste broke the news to them that he'd hit his head and was in the hospital. His mom thanked her and asked her if it was worth making the trip.

"He had brain surgery," Celeste said. "I think I'd come."

The Emmetts were going to take a Lyft, so they weren't even going to bother with her again. And, frankly, the way that Max's mom called her "so well-spoken" at the end of the call, Celeste could give a damn whether she spoke to that condescending, racist lady ever again.

Celeste spent her morning with Marcus. She called up the school early and lied to them, saying he had a dentist appointment and would be there late. The lady in the front office could care less, but Celeste did it because she thought it was funny. Marcus got all scared for a second, thinking that he might really have to go to the dentist. He ran to the bathroom to brush his teeth, and Celeste laughed.

"What good do you think that'll do you now?" she asked him, teasing. At that, he returned from the bathroom, his mouth filled with toothpaste.

"You know Dr. Emmett's sick, right?" Celeste asked her son. "That means you don't have to go to his office. And neither do I. So, what do you want to do?"

Marcus suggested they go to Waffle House, which was a sign that she'd raised him right. So, they had their hash browns all-the-way, their coffees. Marcus had a peanut butter waffle. And they listened to Motown on the jukebox. Smokey Robinson, Diana Ross. Even Michael Jackson. Celeste didn't care about the rumors—and, to her, rumors were all that they would ever be. She just liked the music.

And she loved being with her son, having good and happy moments. Life can be so tough, particularly for boys like Marcus. Every day was some struggle or battle, if you let it be. Celeste wanted to be sure that he had moments where he knew the world was good. She needed that reminder herself this week.

And then, as her son ate, Celeste said what she needed to say.

"Hey Marcus," she said.

"Yeah."

"You know you can talk to me about anything, right?"

"Yes, ma'am."

"Anything."

"Yes."

"Good, I'm glad you know that," she said, then continued before chickening out. "You know your body is yours, right?"

"Huh? I don't know what you mean."

"Your body is yours. No one else can do anything to it without you being OK with it."

Marcus looked confused.

"I want you to know that, if someone tries to touch you or talk you into doing something, if someone makes you uncomfortable, you have every right to stand up for yourself."

"Stand up for myself?"

"If someone tries to hurt you or hit you or threaten you, I want you to yell. I want you to talk about it with someone you trust."

"OK, Mom," he said, concentrating more on his waffle.

"Even if I hurt you in some way," she said, really uncomfortable. "If I accidentally do something that hurts you, I want you to speak up. If a stranger hurts you or someone you know, even someone from the family, I want you to speak up."

"How?"

"I want you to shout. I want you to fight. I want you to know your worth. I want you to demand respect. You deserve to be loved in the right way and on your terms. And if you have to fight, even if you have to fight me, I want you to take care of yourself."

"Why would I have to fight you, Mom?"

She paused for a second, unsure of how to say it. But then she dared to say it the incorrect way, hoping it wouldn't break her child's heart.

"Because sometimes I make mistakes. My momma did with me. Your daddy, sometimes he said and did stuff that hurt me. And I didn't know that I deserved better. So, I want you to know, in case you ever doubt it, that you deserve to be treated well at all times, no matter where you are. You decide where the lines are in your own life, you hear me? And you don't let anybody cross that line unless you're cool with them."

He nodded.

"And you should treat people well. Learn where their lines are. And respect them."

Marcus said, "OK."

"When you talk about things with people, when you talk about sex and love and feelings, that's healthy," Celeste said. "I want you to remember that."

He smiled.

Δ

They took their time, playing song after song, and then they settled the check. And Celeste drove Marcus to school in her Oldsmobile.

If she quit her job, trips like this—even to Waffle House—would have to be budgeted. She'd have to worry about money more. There was no child support. It might take a while to find a job. Max might not even give her a good recommendation if she quit abruptly. But she had to save her soul. She didn't want to be there anymore. She didn't want to look at parents bringing their kids in for a cleaning, wondering each time if Max might go too far again.

This was the moment where Max should've learned a lesson. And maybe he did. But, hell, even if he didn't, Celeste learned one. No amount of money should cost you the ability to look yourself in a mirror. And, for the past months, Celeste hadn't been able to really look at herself, not since Wade started parking that damn Prius outside the office. She'd pretend she didn't see him. She'd not even nod.

Celeste had done him wrong. And it was time to be better.

Right after she dropped Marcus at the school, hugging her boy, reminding him to speak with a slurred voice in case anyone asked him how the visit went, right at 11:15 a.m., Celeste's cell phone rang.

"Hello, I'm trying to reach Celeste Parker," a stern man's voice said to her when she answered.

"This is she."

"We need you to come by Waverly General Hospital," the man said. "We need to update you on Max Emmett's condition. You're listed as his emergency contact."

"I am?"

"The EMTs must've listed that," the hospital man said, audibly rifling through paperwork. "I also have to call Max Emmett's parents."

And, at that, Celeste knew.

"Thank you," she said, then she hung up the phone and headed toward the hospital. The closer she got to the hospital, the harder it was to see the road. In spite of her-self, Celeste shed some tears for her boss.

Δ

When she arrived, Celeste sought out Mary. But the doc-tor insisted upon speaking to her himself.

"Max started having seizures this morning, compli-cations from his injuries, and efforts to revive him just didn't work, I'm sorry," the doctor said. "He passed away at 10:35 a.m."

Thoughts raced through Celeste's head, competing to be the right thing to do in this situation, the right way to react. But Celeste couldn't figure out the best course of action. She knew she could tell the doctor all the things she knew, and she could tell the doctor about what Wade had done. The power to do something, to give Max a sort of justice for being attacked, was there in her grasp. And Max would want justice, Celeste thought, for Max was that arrogant. And she was certainly out of a job now.

She pictured Wade, who was nice and passionate and had no idea how young he was, the hours he spent in that parking lot just waiting. Seeing him there, she should've tapped on his car window and told him to run, that Max was nothing but trouble, that there had been boys like him before.

Celeste decided what justice would look like.

"May I see him, Doctor?" she asked.

The doctor led her from the waiting area of Eight West toward the elevator. As they walked, Celeste glanced down the hallways, toward the nurses' station, trying to catch sight of Mary. But she did not see Wade's mother anywhere.

At the nurses' station, the doctor stopped and grabbed a green plastic bag. He handed it to Celeste.

"These are his things?" she asked.

"They are what the EMTs brought in with them," the doctor said. "His clothes—which are a bit cut up, his shoes, his cell phone."

"You're giving them to me?" Celeste asked.

"Well, you're his emergency contact," the doctor replied. "It's procedure."

The elevator arrived for them. Celeste clutched the bag, then prepared herself to see what was left of him.

Leaving the hospital an hour later, telling the staff that the body and all the arrangements would be handled by Max's parents, Celeste left the bag at the hospital for the Emmetts. It was better that his family have it, anyway. She told the hospital that she was just Max's office manager. She wasn't really his friend.

But Celeste did pocket Max's cell phone before she handed over the bag.

And on Celeste's way to the office, to start delivering the bad news to patients and update her LinkedIn profile, the smartphone—and all its messages from Wade Harrell—suddenly flew out the window of her speeding, beat-up Oldsmobile and into the waters of the Chattahoochee.

Celeste enjoyed the moment. She felt like she was in a Scorsese movie.

CHAPTER TWENTY-NINE

MARY HAD BEEN IN ANOTHER PATIENT'S ROOM WHEN SOMEONE ELSE CALLED THE CODE BLUE FOR MAX THAT MORNING. And when the code team came in to try and revive him, Mary went into Max's room to supposedly help them in any way she could, though she really just wanted to watch his exit. She'd never killed anyone before. She hoped she did it correctly.

After watching them struggle in vain for ten minutes, after they announced to each other that all the lights were off in his sick brain, Mary was sure she had.

He had no one at his side when he died. He had no guests or visitors. It was what he deserved, a lonely death, isolated in his own mind, suffering until he faded.

This had changed her, she realized. She stood back from his hospital bed and watched the shocks jolt through him after his heart stopped. It was weird to enjoy it. But she did enjoy it, kind of a little bit. As a nurse, patients had died on her before. Death wasn't new. Only her participation level had changed.

It's odd acknowledging that you hold that kind of power over someone else and actually using it, she thought. But it's only three short steps from reasonable behavior to murder once you decide to do it.

226

She decided she didn't care about the consequences enough to stop.

She determined how to do it.

And she willed herself forward past any internal objection.

Murder was easier than she thought. Mary didn't know why people didn't do it more often.

And then she considered that maybe they do, maybe people get away with murder all the time. Not just figuratively, either, like politicians or the rich "get away with murder." Every day, people could be doing what she had done and just not gotten caught. Maybe the way that bad things happen so regularly, like domestic violence and child molestation, was that people just didn't talk about it and pretended like everything was normal. Maybe every bad thing is commonplace, but everyone buries it. Because of that, every bad thing that happens, every person feels like they're alone.

What a fucked way to consider the world, she thought. It's so fucked that it's probably accurate.

Mary was a murderer now. But she had no way of knowing if she was the only murderer in this room or any room.

She could kill again if she needed to. So then, she whispered to herself, "Please, please, never need to."

The doctor glanced over to her, looking Mary in the eye, and said something to her.

"What?" she asked him.

"I was saying the time of death," he replied. "What were you whispering?"

"Oh, nothing," Mary replied.

In the next few minutes, the orderlies took Max to the morgue. The doctors said they'd call the family and the emergency contacts. And Mary, in a daze of sorts because nothing mattered, really, told her supervisor that she was going home.

"I came in early to cover for Jasmine," Mary said to her. "Have a nice weekend."

It was Friday. It was just Friday. The dentist had been in her care for one day. In one day, Mary felt like she'd aged five years.

Arriving home, Mary found a note from Wade, telling her he'd picked up an early work shift, too.

"May as well take advantage of the suspension," he wrote. "Love, Wade." He wrote "Love." They were going to be all right.

Mary didn't call him about Max or text him the news. Better to wait, she thought. It's the sort of thing he'd handle better in person. Wade was terrible dealing with stress.

She grabbed her phone, called her old therapist Julia's office, asked if Julia worked with children and set the earliest appointment possible for her son. The receptionist at Julia's office asked Mary if she wanted an appointment herself while they were at it.

"No, I'm good," Mary said, chuckling. She hung up the phone. Then she went upstairs and took a shower.

Under her kitchen sink were the gloves, so Mary got down on her knees in her bathrobe, rifled her way past the bucket of cleaning supplies and grabbed herself a fresh yellow pair. She closed the cabinet beneath the sink. With ease, she slid the large, loose gloves over her hands.

Then she stood up, slid her butt on to the counter with a push. She maneuvered her way on to her knees again, reached up over the refrigerator and opened that cabinet—Wade's secret cabinet. The smile greeted her as she opened the door, the gleaming white of the ceramic, braced teeth shining from the darkness. She pulled the heavy model jaw into the light and looked it over for dust and hair. There were a few traces on the front teeth.

The jaw was substantial and beautiful, probably a gift to Max after he'd graduated from dental school. Most of the medical models that Mary saw in her job were all plastic, hollow, easy to take apart. Max's teeth were hinged and metal, probably something from the 1960s.

Whomever had given it to Max had loved him, had been proud of him.

That was difficult to consider, that someone was going to miss Max, someone who knew him from the time he was a kid, someone who maybe didn't know that he was a monstrous sort. Or maybe they didn't care he was a monster.

Max had a mother somewhere, a mother who wouldn't rest if she feared any harm had come to her son, Mary thought.

Max's mother could never know what happened, Mary determined. No one could ever know.

She placed the teeth on the counter, lowered her legs to the floor and stood in front of the sink. She turned on the faucet, let the water flow until it was steaming up the kitchen window.

And, using dish soap and a spare toothbrush, Mary cleaned the teeth. And the braces. And the jawbone. Thoroughly. Extensively. And then again. And again. Until there were no traces of the dead man, her son or herself left on them. And she wrapped them in a towel.

Then looking around the pantry, Mary found an empty Oster box that the rice cooker had come home in, and she placed the mouth inside it.

As a final step, she carried the boxed teeth out to the porch and placed them in the larger box of Jessa's belongings.

Δ

Two hours later, Rev. Lancaster knocked on the front door. And Mary, still in a bathrobe because the only thing she'd managed to do was remove the gloves and put them in the trash until she just froze there in the kitchen, processing all of her actions and her feelings about her actions and what actions might be left to do and all the things that she maybe hadn't considered, answered the door and just nodded to the man.

"Is this everything, Mrs. Harrell?" he asked her, holding the box.

"Where's Jessa?" she asked, able to find words, the first ones she'd said aloud in hours. "She's at school," Rev. Lancaster said.

"And the baby? Did you leave her in your car or something?"

"The church daycare," he said. "Jessa asked me to stop by and grab her stuff."

"Asked you or told you?" Mary asked.

"You know Jessa," he sighed.

"Yes."

Mary smiled.

"How was your first night with the baby?" Mary asked, then she turned familiar. "You look like hell, Eric."

"I had forgotten what it was like, having a baby in the house."

"You and Rachel must've had your hands full," Mary said, smirking.

"Oh, Rachel wouldn't even hold the baby."

"She what—?"

"Yeah," he said. "She wouldn't even talk to Jessa when we got home. Rachel said she had a migraine, didn't acknowledge the baby at all and locked herself in the bedroom all night."

"And where'd you sleep?"

"With a two-month-old in a strange house, surrounded by new faces and terrified, perpetually crying and screaming, I didn't sleep anywhere, Mary."

Mary laughed. She found she could laugh. He was holding the box. It would be over soon. She could laugh.

Mary eyed Rev. Lancaster warmly. It startled the man.

"You can bring the baby back whenever you like, Eric," she told him sweetly, then changed tone. "But you can keep your goddamn daughter."

Irked at her insult, he repeated his question as she held on to the door. "Is this box everything?"

"I think so," she said to him. And then she shut the door in his face.

CHAPTER THIRTY

WADE'S SHIFT ENDED JUST AFTER 2 P.M., AND HE DIDN'T KNOW WHAT TO DO WITH HIMSELF. There was no baby at home, no girlfriend watching "Riverdale" in his basement, no after-school project that he was allowed to attend, no dentist waiting to talk to him in a parking lot. His day was free. And so, free from obligation, he considered working a double shift.

But he was too tired for that. The week had exhausted him. He took out his phone and texted Trevor, "You free?"

Almost immediately, Wade saw that the text was read at 2:07 p.m., then he saw the three dots indicating that a reply was coming. And then, without payoff, the three dots just disappeared. So, Wade just got into his Prius and sat there. He considered tracking down where Lydie was, seeing her and cuddling with her. But seeing Lydie meant maybe seeing Jessa or her dad. And he didn't want to do that.

The hole in the window was too startling. Suddenly, Wade had a problem to fix, and life was so much clearer when he had something or someone to distract him. So, he started the car up and drove until he found a body shop.

The clerk there told him that it could all be fixed by Monday, if he wanted to leave it there over the weekend.

The Prius reminded him of Dr. Emmett. He didn't want that kind of reminder. Wade left the keys on the counter and walked outside.

Maybe it was OK to have moments where you are by yourself, Wade thought. It seemed novel. He took a breath.

Then he checked his phone to see if Trevor had written anything back yet. And Trevor had not.

Instead, Wade summoned a Lyft. For a moment, he thought about getting a coffee by himself. And then he considered going back to the hospital, sitting with Dr. Emmett for a bit and having another one of their talks. The sedation had made Max a really great listener.

But Wade set his destination for home. He put in his earbuds and listened to more of that audiobook. Even when the car arrived, Wade didn't speak to the driver. He just listened more to that audiobook about being a positive and effective person out in the world.

The author made it sound like hard work with little reward and no clear, certain way to make life any easier.

Wade hoped to find the solution for himself. Age 17 had been absolutely terrible so far.

Δ

He walked in the front door to his house, hoping to watch TV in the living room and maybe get his mom to cook something for him. Jessa's box was already off the porch, so Wade had dodged that bullet.

"Did Jessa bring Lydie when she got her stuff?" he asked his mom.

Mary was sitting at the kitchen table, looking intently at him under the soft lights. She pulled out a chair for him, then motioned for him to come sit down. Everything at that table lately had been so dreadful and emotional, and Wade couldn't take another talk there.

"Can you just tell me what happened now?" he asked his mom. "Do I have to sit there again for another heart-to-heart?"

Mary's eyes flashed with anger at her son, and Wade realized immediately he'd been too glib.

"Sorry," he said to her.

"The dentist is dead," she said to him curtly,

Wade looked at her, the words passing over him like Teflon.

"Did you hear me?" she asked. "The dentist died this morning."

"Wait, what?"

"Honey, Dr. Emmett passed away."

"But he was awake yesterday," Wade told his mother, his voice getting smaller with every word. "You told me that he was going to make it."

"These things sometimes take a turn for the worse," Mary said. "I'm sorry."

"Stop it," Wade said, panicking. "This isn't funny, Mom."

"I know it isn't."

Wade rushed to check his phone.

"You said it happened this morning? You didn't call me!"

"I wanted to tell you in person," she said, her voice detached. "There wasn't anything you could've done for him. Dr. Emmett just started convulsing and then faded away."

Wade glared at her. "Are you enjoying this?"

"I haven't enjoyed any of this," she said to him. "But I don't think it's that much of a tragedy. I can't lie about that."

Wade trembled, caught somewhere between sadness and fear.

"What are you feeling, Wade?" his mother asked him. Both her eyes and his eyes looked to the cabinet above the refrigerator.

"I murdered him," Wade whispered to her. "Oh my God, I murdered him."

With that, she rose from the table and went to embrace her son.

"You're no murderer, Wade," she said to him. "That man was a child molester and a monster."

"I hit him over the head, Mom. I killed him." She hugged him. He let her.

"You didn't."

"How in the hell am I not a murderer, Mom? I should just turn myself in."

"You're not a murderer, Wade."

"That nurse Celeste, she's going to tell them what I did. She knows what I did. She knows about everything. Maybe if I just—Mom, how could I have done this to him?"

Mary paused, considered what to answer first.

"You're not a murderer, Wade," she repeated more firmly.

"I thought I loved him, Mom," Wade said. "How could I do this to him?"

"Wade, I know you don't believe this, but that man tricked you and manipulated you. He did what he did to you over and over to lots of boys like you."

Wade let his mother hold him a moment. Then, he squirmed out of her grasp. He went to the kitchen counter and hoisted himself up. Mary tried to stop him.

"I'm going to take these, and I'm going to the police," he said. "I can't live with this." Wade climbed up and opened the secret cabinet. The teeth were no longer there.

"Where are they?" he asked his mother.

"I took care of it," Mary said to Wade.

"What are you talking about?" he asked her, aghast.

"You're not a murderer, Wade," she repeated to him, staring up at him on the counter. "I took care of it."

His face turned white. He knew where the teeth were without having to ask her.

"That girl always wants a life like a soap opera," Mary said to him, colder than she had ever sounded before. "If Jessa tries to take Lydie away from me, I can make her life very, very dramatic."

Wade climbed down off the counter, his eyes glaring deep into his mother's steely gaze.

"You can't involve Jessa in this," Wade said. "She doesn't know anything about the dentist. She doesn't know anything about what I've been up to. She's never met the man before." Mary smirked at her son.

"And that's what she can tell the police if anyone ever starts asking questions about her boyfriend's boyfriend," she said. "But, for right now, everybody just thinks the man fell down."

Wade looked at his mother, terrified of how far she was willing to go.

"Let's just act like he fell down," Mary said to her son, not daring to tell him anything more about her morning, not telling him how far she really went. "It would save everyone a lot of grief."

Wade sat at the table, put his head in his hands and started crying—for Max, for himself and for the mess that he wanted so badly to be over.

"Don't cry, Wade," his mother said. "That man isn't worth the trouble."

Suddenly, Wade got up and bolted from the house. He didn't want to be in the same room as his mother. He had to get away. He had to go anywhere. But once he reached the porch, he remembered that his Prius wasn't in the driveway.

His phone was still inside. He was low on funds, anyway. Wade had nowhere to go, except back inside the house.

Mary's eyes went from a glare to something warmer. He took a breath at the familiar sight. He needed his mother. He didn't want to be without her, even if she was just as messed up as every other person he knew.

"I'm sorry about everything, Wade," she whispered to him, pulling him into another hug.

"I'm sorry, too," he said to her. "This was all my fault."

She loosened her grip on him a moment.

"It's not all on you, Wade," she said, patting his shoulder gently. She had a weird look on her face, Wade thought. And then she continued her thought.

"Frankly, I blame the dentist for most of the trouble," his mother said.

CHAPTER THIRTY-ONE

ON MONDAY MORNING, WADE WORE A GRAY SUIT WITH A BLACK TIE AND AN IVORY POCKET SQUARE, LOOKING DAPPER AND MATURE. At least, that's what his mom told him.

"I don't know that you need to get all dressed up for this, Wade," Mary said as they got into her Yaris. "It's not like Dr. Emmett can see you."

Wade thought to himself that the outfit wasn't for Dr. Emmett's benefit. That game was over.

The suit—which was one of his dad's old ones—meant something else to Wade. To go to an adult event in his life, Wade tried on adult clothes, and the adult clothes fit him. That part mattered to Wade, as he focused on all that the day would bring.

The fact that he looked like a million bucks while attending his ex's funeral, presided over by his other ex's disapproving father, was just a bonus.

"You sure you don't want to come with me to this thing?" Wade asked his mother, who scoffed a little but kept her eyes on the road.

"No, honey, I've said my goodbyes."

There was a silence after that. It grew more and more awkward with each mile until Mary mercifully put on her radio. Some jazz song was playing, light piano and a mournful saxophone.

"What's this?" Wade asked his mother, but one glance at the radio let him know that the song was "In a Sentimental Mood."

Wade leaned his head back against the seat and closed his eyes. Within minutes, Mary had pulled up to their destination and nudged Wade.

"This is your stop," she said to him. "Let me know how it goes today." They were at the body shop. Wade's blue Prius had a new window.

He got out of her car and shut the door, mouthing to her that he would be in touch.

Mary nodded and headed toward the hospital.

Within a few minutes, Wade had paid for the repairs and received his keys again. He looked at his phone to check the time. It was 9:30 a.m. The funeral was at 11 a.m. His other appointment was at 1 p.m.

Wade got into his Prius, started the ignition and, as usual, heard nothing. The car that had been through so much remained silent about most of it. Wade figured he should follow its example once he arrived at the church. It only took ten minutes to reach the destination.

Instead of sitting and waiting in the parking lot, Wade got out of the Prius and walked inside the church. He walked past the sanctuary and past Rev. Lancaster's office, not stopping until he arrived at the daycare.

Wade motioned to one of the workers to get her attention, then smiled.

"Jessa Lancaster should've left a message with you this morning when she dropped off Lydie," Wade whispered gently to the woman. "She and I talked this week-end about it. I told her I would be here."

The daycare worker brightened. "Yes sir," she said.

Then she disappeared into the nursery for a min-ute, then returned with Lydie, all wrapped up in a little pink blanket, gently fussy. But once Lydie was in Wade's arms, looking into his eyes, she stopped crying. Wade smiled at his little girl. The daycare worker handed Wade a bottle, then she left the father and daughter alone for a while.

Δ

The funeral for Max Emmett was small. His parents sat in the front row, dressed in black and looking unaffect-ed. Max's uncle sat with them. His face was pale, and he looked stunned.

There was a smattering of other friends, little pock-ets of folks gathered in the pews. There was some mut-tering before the service started, but most of the faces seemed anxious to get it over with, from what Wade could see.

Max's body had been cremated, per his personal wishes. Wade knew from his mother's connections that there had been no autopsy.

Before the service started, Wade, sitting in the aisle by himself in a row closer to the back, felt a tap-tap-tap on his shoulder. He turned and saw, as he expected, Ce-leste, the only person who would talk to him at this mo-ment.

She squeezed his shoulder and whispered to him kindly, "How you doing, baby? You all right?"

"I'm fine," Wade whispered back.

"Really?" she asked, a little too surprised.

"Yeah, I thought it might be weird to come to this," Wade said. "But it felt—I don't know—it felt like the right thing to do."

"I get you," Celeste whispered.

"How about you?" he asked her. They were friends now, he guessed.

"I think I'll be OK," Celeste said. "Max's business insurance is going to cover my paycheck for a little while. His parents just told me that a little bit ago, which is cool because I was in a little bit of a panic."

"Oh?" Wade asked.

"Yeah, apparently he had a plan in place for sudden death."

Wade turned in his pew to look in Celeste's eyes. Sometimes, that woman's words had layers.

"Is that a joke?" Wade asked her.

"I don't make jokes at funerals," she said.

Then she startled Wade by getting up and moving herself to his pew, motioning for him to scooch over. He followed her command. Celeste sat down next to him. She was wearing a nice black dress with white gardenias in the pattern.

She leaned in and whispered in his ear, "You're not the only one of his boys to come to this. Did you notice that?"

Wade turned to her with a start.

"What?" he asked, his tone a little higher.

Celeste nodded toward another skinny young man, blond, probably about 17.

"That's Christopher," she said. "He used to come by the office all the time for cleanings a couple years back. I had no idea what was happening then. But look at him. He's being all weird."

Wade looked at the boy's manner. Christopher was trembling, looking mostly down at the program. His leg kept twitching nervously.

Celeste then directed Wade's attention a few pews behind them. Wade turned briefly to consider the young man, then turned quickly around.

"Jacob Myers," Celeste said to Wade. "He's younger than you are. He was last year, I think. I can't be sure. But he switched dentists. I mean, why would you come to your old dentist's wake?"

Wade was stunned, unsure what to think, until Celeste filled in the blanks for him.

"I'm sorry I showed him that video, Wade," she said. "I didn't mean to get you mixed up with that man. I should've done better by you."

Wade stared ahead. He couldn't look at her.

"It's good that Max is gone, Wade," she said. "Don't you worry."

Trying to figure out anything to say, Wade just muttered, "I'm sorry you're out of a job." Celeste just sighed.

"I'll find work, Wade," she said. "There are lots of other dentists."

Δ

The service was done quickly. Rev. Lancaster really didn't know Dr. Emmett well enough to say much beyond the usual psalms. And the Emmetts didn't do any readings. The whole thing lasted maybe 20 minutes before Rev. Lancaster invited anyone who wanted to share memories of Max up to the front of the sanctuary to share.

Awkwardly, no one rose to say anything in memoriam.

The silence surprised Rev. Lancaster, who kept asking "Anyone?" for 45 agonizing seconds. For a moment, Wade and the reverend made eye contact. The reverend looked puzzled, and, from the pulpit, his mouth started to ask Wade a question like "What are you doing here?" But Wade looked down before the question even formed, avoiding the minister's consideration.

Wade had nothing to say about Max. After parting words, Rev. Lancaster told everyone that coffee and snacks would be available in the fellowship hall.

Wade arrived at the therapist Julia's office at 12:45 p.m. to fill out the paperwork. He had the insurance information that his mother had copied for him so that he could attend the appointment alone. The gray suit made the receptionist and the other people in the waiting area treat him like a grown-up, which made him smile.

He went to the Keurig station and grabbed a chamomile pod and some Splenda. He wanted to make sure he was at his calmest before meeting this lady. Then he sat and filled out the forms himself.

At 1:04 p.m., a couple exited Julia's counseling room, and Wade grew a little bit anxious. He had no idea what to tell this person. Like, where would he even start? His temper? The baby? The dentist? The murder stuff?

Julia poked her head out of the counseling room.

"Wade Harrell?" she asked. He nodded.

"You ready?"

Wade rose from the chair and entered the room, which was softly lit with lots of lamps and had a lot of full bookshelves. Wade had expected there to be a couch, like the cliché he'd seen on TV, but there were lots of places to sit, not just couches.

"The room's a bit big," Julia said to him. "I use it for group therapy sometimes. But I find that it gives people options, as well. Do you want to sit by the window?"

Wade said he didn't care, then selected a comfy chair by the window. Julia sat opposite him and smiled. She was a thirtysomething brunette lady in a baggy pink sweater and a long skirt. She flipped to a blank page in her notebook and wrote down his name and the date. She seemed nice. But Wade figured that was probably the point.

"So, Wade," Julia began.

"Yeah?"

"What brings you here today?"

"I don't know," Wade said. "My mom made this appointment."

"Do you want to be here?"

He paused.

"Yeah," Wade said.

"Well, why do you want to be here?" Julia asked him.

Wade considered for a moment everything that had bugged him, everything that he had been through. He missed his dad. He didn't feel in control. Wade had been at Jessa's and Max's disposal, and he was tired and confused. He just turned 17, and everything was already chaos. And it had to stop. All of the chaos had to stop. Wade had to find some way. He looked in the therapist's eyes.

"I want to survive," he said.

THE END

Δ

ACKNOWLEDGMENTS

It took me a long time to get here, and I'm surprised this is happening. Granted, since living with a disability is slow-going and life in general is treacherous, I could maybe say that every time I walk into a room or have a new experience. But I have wanted to have a book published with my name on the cover, shelved alphabetically in a library or bookstore, since I first read *Ramona the Brave* and realized that Beverly Cleary had my initials. Since then, the dream lingered in the back of my head, feeling so impossible sometimes that it was hard to keep hold of it amid doubts and insecurity.

When you don't see yourself as remarkable, it is useful to surround yourself with people who believe in your strengths more than you do. My parents and my brother Dan believed in my talents and nurtured them, from buying me *Ramona* books to listening to me ramble for hours when I couldn't ever make a simple decision without endless, soul-crushing worrying. My thanks have to start with them. They earned dibs.

Of course, when praise comes from your family, it isn't easy to believe—particularly if your brain is unfair to you. (My brain was very unkind when I was a teenager, and it still can be.) To combat that, I recommend that you surround yourself with other supportive people. Maybe they like you. Maybe they like your work. Maybe they see your potential. They are the ones who will demand that you stick around long enough to give them hugs, share that coffee or finish that story. The love of others helps combat the doubts you may have about your own worth.

I met my best friend Vickye Shotton in high school, and the value that she has added to my life and work is beyond measure. For ages, she has been the first and most important reader of any new story I've tried. She makes me a better person and a better artist with every conversation. Her friendship enriches my life. Her notes enrich my work. This novel happened because of her.

Special thanks go to her mom Donna Shotton, as well, for her nursing expertise. I couldn't have killed a guy without her.

Thanks to Jessica Nettles, Carrie Gibson, Nathan Brown, Gregg van Laningham, Jared van Aalten, Nathan Spicer, Jason Morin, Richard Nenoff, Justin Barisich, Mauree Culberson, Josh McTeer, Alayna Huft Tucker, Lisa Hunt Kuebler, Bran Peacock, Carmen Tanner Slaughter, Crystal O'Leary-Davidson and Daniel Lamb for their attention as this work developed.

For their love and friendship, thanks to Stephen Wilczak, JD Dreiling, Blake Ussery, Lacee Aderhold, Bryan Edwards, Jennifer Resendez, Gary Anthony, Jonathan Lupo, Kenn Archibald, Samantha Carr, Shannon Carr, Holly Kessler, Trista Todt, Greg and Tara Lineweaver, Hyuna Sung, Debbie and Cleve Stanfield, Katherine George, Bryan and Anna Pritchett, Chris Stanford, Holly Steel, Vicki Franch, C.J. Spraggins, Elizabeth Perry, Christina Gentry, Steven Igarashi-Ball and Dena Beck.

Special thanks to Jon Carr, Randy Osborne, Joyce Mitchell, Theresa Davis, Jon Goode, Will Young, Katie Steenerson, Ashley Robinson, Ian Campbell, Ben Bowlin, Brandi Supra, Nicki Salcedo, Lauren Vogelbaum, Jerad Alexander, Nicholas Tecosky, Myke Johns, Gina Rickicki, Bernard Setaro Clark, Jack Walsh, Dani Herd, David Bruckner, Tricia Stearns, Michael Henry Harris, Samantha Thomson LoCoco, Daniel and Kate Guyton, Celeste Campbell, Adam and Angela Kaylor, Jyll Thomas, Liesel Sloan, Miles Cliatt, Arian Gulick, Claire Christie, Jeremiah Prescott, Michael Haverty, Dave Ferris, Pat Young, Suehyla El-Attar, Amber Nash, George Faughnan, Z Gillispie, Matt Horgan, Randy Havens, Ed Morgan, Tom Rittenhouse, Rueben Medina, Diana Lancaster, Alex Ridgeway, David Russell, Winston Blake Wheeler Ward, Joanie Drago, Joe Davich, Scott Gassman, Denise Mount and Sarah Beth Nelson. I am grateful to call the Atlanta arts community my home.

Bonus points go to the Dunkin Donuts on North Druid Hills Road, where I wrote this.

Topher Payne is a wonderful friend and a tremendous artist. Thank you for your love and for designing my book cover.

Thanks to Brian Panowich, Katy Miles, Grant Jerkins, Larry Corse, Conrad Fink, Richard Neupert, Tray Butler, Sarah Shope, Latoya Smith, Stephen Lee and Emily Giffin for the encouragement.

Thank you to Elaine Cleveland, Anne Day, Pat Nash, Gail Aiken, Marjorie Wilson, Chris Fowler, Ashley Newman, Bonnie Davis and Debbie Hall—and my hometown of Buford—for teaching me valuable lessons. Thank you to my friends at the Phi Kappa Literary Society and The Red & Black for transforming my entire life's path at the University of Georgia.

The Broadleaf Writers Association is a wonderful, inspiring organization, and I am grateful to be a part of it. The annual Broadleaf Writers Conference changed my life. *Impacted* is in front of you because of the encouragement and friendship of Zachary Steele.

Finally, without the time and attention of John Adcox and Lou Aronica, from Gramarye Media and The Story Plant, a rough draft of this novel would be collecting dust at the bottom of a desk drawer. Instead, thanks to you, it's on a shelf with the likes of Beverly Cleary, though probably in a much different section than *Ramona the Brave*.

Much gratitude,

Benji Carr
Oct. 12, 2020

ABOUT THE AUTHOR

As a child growing up in the South with cerebral palsy, Benji Carr developed an eye for the bizarre and quirky, which provided all of the stories he told his friends and family with a bit of flavor. Working as a journalist, storyteller and playwright, his work—whether the stories be personal tales of struggle and survival or fiction about cannibal lunch ladies, puppet romances, drag queen funerals, and perverted killer circus clowns—has been featured in *The Guardian*, *ArtsATL* and *Pembroke Magazine*. Onstage, his pieces have been presented at the Center for Puppetry Arts, Alliance Theatre, and as part of the Samuel French Off-Off Broadway Short Play Festival in Manhattan. He lives in Atlanta and helps run the online literary magazine, *Gutwrench Journal*. *Impacted* is his first novel.